In the latest story of the Elder Races, two mates face their deadliest challenge yet—each other...

Pia and Dragos' magical young son Liam (the Peanut), is growing at an unprecedented rate, and if that isn't enough, he is also exhibiting new, and unpredictable, magical gifts. To protect him, the concerned parents decide to move to upstate New York.

Both Dragos and Pia relish the idea of leaving behind the city. They finally have the space to indulge their Wyr side, and Liam can grow in safety. It's a breath of fresh air—literally—but their idyllic situation is shattered when Dragos is injured in a freak accident.

Stripped of his memory and bereft of Pia's taming influence, there's nothing holding back Dragos's darkest side. And in order to restore her family and save her mate, Pia must confront the most powerful menace in Elder Races history.

It's going to take more than a penny to fix this...

Pia Saves the Day is part of a three-story series about Pia, Dragos, and Peanut. Each story stands alone, but fans might want to read all three: *Dragos Takes a Holiday*, *Pia Saves the Day*, and *Peanut Goes to School*.

Pia Saves the Day

Thea Harrison

Pia Saves the Day
Copyright © 2014 by Teddy Harrison LLC
ISBN-10: 0989972860
ISBN-13: 978-0-9899728-6-4
Print Edition

To all my wonderful, supportive author friends,
especially Courtney, Vivian, Bree and Libby,
all of whom have been so generous with sharing
their knowledge, opinions and experience.
And to my assistant Janine, who has embraced this crazy
lifestyle with such enthusiasm.

Chapter One

PIA FLUFFED HER new haircut as Eva turned their SUV onto the long drive that led up to the house. When Pia realized she was still distancing herself from claiming the sprawling mansion as her own, she made a deliberate choice to change the wording in her head.

Their house—*her* house—was located in upstate New York, nestled in two hundred acres of land that contained virgin forest and a lake with water so clean and clear, it sparkled like a blue jewel in the sun.

While the estate was beautiful, she found it surprisingly hard to stake an emotional claim to it, but hopefully that would change with all of the renovations, when the house truly became her home.

"Stop fussing," Eva said. "Or you're gonna mess it up."

"I can't help it," she muttered, even as she forced herself to drop her hands into her lap. "I've never had my hair cut this short before, and it feels weird."

The summer had been a whirlwind of activity, and it was still only July. After they vacationed in Bermuda—a trip that had been full of wonderful moments and unexpected stresses—they went straight into the annual political season that surrounded the summer solstice. Amidst parties, meetings and other inter-demesne functions that were attended by representatives of all the Elder Races, Dragos and his sentinels had worked double time to make sure all the sentinels got their promised time off.

At the same time, he and Pia set in motion plans to move upstate, build personal quarters for staff and an office complex, and completely redo the large mansion on the estate.

Meanwhile, Peanut kept growing, growing, growing. Because both his parents held such rare forms of Power, Dragos said he was springing into existence in a way that was reminiscent of the first of the Elder Races, at Earth's dawning.

Peanut's journey was not quite the same—at the birth of the world, magic had been wild and prolific, and the first-generation Elders had not gone through any childhood phase. Still, it had become more than apparent their son would not live any kind of ordinary life. While he was only four months old, he had already reached the size of a very precocious toddler, and it took everything Pia had to try to keep up with him.

From one day to the next, her patience snapped with the upkeep involved in taking care of her waist-length hair. It had to go.

Now the bottom of her new hairstyle touched her shoulders, and it was layered throughout. She had lost so much hair, she felt almost light-headed, and the ends tickled her collarbones as she turned her head from side to side.

She was very pleased with how the feminine style suited her triangular face, and it felt so much cooler, she was already in love with it.

However, she hadn't told Dragos she was getting her hair cut, and now she was starting to feel nervous. There was no way she would ever ask him for *permission* to cut her own hair—the very thought was outrageous—but she also knew he loved her long hair, and … well, she wanted him to like how she looked.

"It's perfect," Eva told her.

She smiled. "Thanks."

As they followed the drive that curved around a copse of trees, the house came into view, surrounded by scaffolding, more than twenty vehicles, an array of heavy construction tractors, and piles of building supplies. The nearby town's single motel remained perpetually booked, and a hundred yards away from the main house, several trailers housed even more workers, along with providing temporary quarters for any of the sentinels who chose to visit the estate, which happened often.

The sentinels claimed any number of excuses for coming—the need to talk over business with Dragos in person, the desire to help out—but Pia suspected they were all just excited at the change in lifestyle, and they enjoyed the opportunity to get out of the city.

Once construction was completed, the sentinels would go on rotation, so that at any given time, two would be headquartered upstate. Dragos believed the new system would help prevent burnout and give the sentinels a chance to stretch their wings—or, in Quentin's case, legs.

For now, the scene looked bustling and chaotic, and it wouldn't calm down for at least another two months. Close by, sounds of construction echoed off the surface of the lake. In a series of small explosions, the construction crew was blasting through a stubborn shelf of bedrock to level the site where the office complex would be built. Periodically the low boom from the blasts rolled over the valley like cannon fire.

After Eva parked, they climbed out of the air-conditioned vehicle into the sultry heat of the day.

Another thunderous boom sounded in the distance. Pia felt it vibrate in her chest, and she sighed. "I can't wait for them to be done with that."

"Yeah, it got old fast, didn't it?" Eva swept the scene with her gaze. A haze of dust lay over the tree line in the direction of the noise. "At least they should be finished with the blasting by the end of the week."

As they reached the open front doorway, they met several workmen coming out. Pia stepped aside to let them pass, returning cheerful greetings and smiling when one of them complimented her new look.

When the path was clear, Eva left her to head to the kitchen for some lunch, and Pia went in search of Dragos and Liam. Stepping around ladders, cans of paint and drop cloths, she made her way through the house to the back.

While the rest of the estate was in upheaval, and construction dust seemed to coat everything, Pia and Dragos had finished a few areas before they had ever made the trip upstate. Their bedroom suite, Peanut's rooms, the rooms for essential household staff, like Eva and Hugh, along with the back patio areas and the kitchen had been completely redone. With the basics of survival sorted out, Pia felt like they could withstand anything.

At the back of the house, French doors opened to the large patio. Comfortable outside furniture with deep cushions dotted the open expanse. To one side, wide shallow steps led to an area created for open-air dining, with a spacious brick grill, an outdoor oven and a dining table and chairs.

To the other side, steps led to a sparkling, inground heated pool and pool house, surrounded by a decorative, black iron safety fence. Pia had to smile as she looked around with pleasure and satisfaction. Blooming bushes and flowerbeds surrounded the patio areas, and beyond that, a massive green lawn rolled gently downhill to the bordering forest.

Next week, work crews would build a security fence around that lawn, along with a large wooden play set, complete with a sandpit. Of course, neither the security fence nor the pool safety fence could contain Liam if he chose to change into his Wyr form and fly over them, but after what had happened in Bermuda, he had only been shapeshifting when he needed to feed his dragon form or when he was taken on a supervised flight.

Still, none of them could predict how long Liam's obedient streak would last. After his adventures in Bermuda, Pia and Dragos had hired two extra avian nannies to fill in for when Pia was needed elsewhere. Along with Hugh, his new caretakers, Sasha and Ryssa, watched him like the hawks they were.

Pia looked wryly at her precocious, magical son, currently curled on Dragos's chest.

In the sitting area on the patio, Dragos sprawled on a lounge chair large enough to support his powerful, six-foot-eight frame. He wore jeans, boots and a white T-shirt. As he wasn't the kind of man to stand back while watching others work, his current outfit had already seen some wear and tear. Since they had come upstate, he had already demolished several pairs of jeans and shirts. Stacks of papers, manila folders and a laptop lay on a table pulled close to the right side of his chair, and toys lay scattered on the floor.

Peanut was fast asleep, and his thumb had fallen halfway out of his small, slack mouth. Wisps of his white blond hair fluttered in the gentle summer breeze.

His father read aloud, quietly, his voice steady and gentle, while he pressed a hand to Liam's delicate back, supporting his position. The bracelet Dragos had made from her braided hair last year glinted gold on the dark bronze skin of his thick, strong wrist.

Whenever she saw Dragos with Liam, a tangled well of emotion overcame Pia—a great, fierce storm of love. This time the emotional storm was mingled with a thread of laughter, as she realized Dragos was reading the quarterly profit percentages from a stockholders' report.

A snort escaped her nose. It was a small sound, amidst all the bustle and noise of the day, but Dragos's head lifted, and he turned to look at her.

His expression changed drastically and he surged to his feet, all in one smooth flowing motion that never disturbed the sleeping toddler he cradled in one arm.

He demanded telepathically, *Where's the rest of it?*

She knew immediately what he meant. One fact of their life would never change—her Wyr form was unique enough, they must always be careful to destroy any trace of her blood, and both Power and dangerous information could be gleaned from hair and nail clippings.

Giving him a reassuring smile, she told him, *Eva swept the floor and made sure she got all the clippings. I've got it right here.*

Reaching into her purse, she pulled out a paper bag that held the hair she had lost with the new hairstyle.

Dragos's tension eased. *Okay.*

Then he tilted his head, lids lowering over gold eyes as he regarded her, and his expression underwent a subtle, sensual change. Strolling over to her, he slid his free hand underneath the hair at the nape of her neck. Gently, gently, he took a fistful and tilted her head back.

Hot and fierce arousal pooled in her lower body, sweeping inescapably over her like slow-moving lava. As she stared up at him, her lips parted, and her breathing changed and grew ragged. He did this to her every time, so effortlessly, like striking a match. He could claim her with a glance, a touch, a simple shift of his cruel-looking, sexy lips, and when he did, she went up in flames. Every time, everywhere.

Not too short. His telepathic voice was a mere growl of

a whisper that swept over her nerve endings in an intimate caress. While everything they did together was sexy, there was absolutely nothing sexier than having him in her head. *I can still grab a good handful. I like it.*

I hoped you would, she said, her own telepathic voice unsteady.

Dragos bent his head and kissed her, softly because their sleeping son nestled between them. His firm, warm lips parted hers, and he dipped his tongue into her mouth in an erotic promise for later. Awash in the lava that burned through her veins, she steadied herself by gripping his bicep. With obvious reluctance, he pulled away.

In the fourteen months they had been together, the desire had never changed. Elemental, as necessary as breathing, it dictated the rhythm of their lives. They orbited around each other, always looking, always reaching for the other, but it never ceased to amaze her that *he* looked at her this way.

His brutally handsome face could be so hard, so ruthless, but his need for her always won through. She never doubted what he felt for her. She could see it in everything he did.

You want me, she breathed.

She'd meant to say it in a cocky and flirtatious way, with a wink and a saucy Marilyn Monroe wiggle of the hips. But she forgot to wink, the hip wiggle turned into a slow, needy roll against his, and the words came out breathless and awed.

He rubbed the calloused ball of his thumb across her

soft, moistened lips. A dark flush stained his high cheekbones, and his gold eyes glittered. *I'll die before I stop wanting you.*

Me too. She closed her eyes at his touch.

They were both immortal Wyr. Maybe, just maybe, that would be long enough to express the depth of what she felt for him.

He kissed her forehead. *Here, take Liam.*

Coming back to herself, she held open her arms, and he gently transferred the sleeping boy over to her. Liam half roused, gave her a sleepy, confused look and smiled. "Mama," he remarked happily. "Mamamamamama."

So far, it was his favorite and only spoken word. Patting her with a small hand, he laid his head on her shoulder and fell back asleep with the abrupt abandonment of extreme youth.

Dragos took the paper bag that held her hair and strode over to the dining area. When he reached the brick grill, he set the bag down on it and his gold eyes flared with incandescence. Cradling Liam as she watched, she felt the small, hot surge of his Power from where she stood. The paper bag, along with its contents, burst into flames.

Dragos didn't move until the flames had burned out. Afterward, he blew on the white flakes of ash until they had dispersed entirely. Only then did he walk back to her.

"How was your trip into town?" he asked.

Located a short drive away from the estate, the town boasted a main street and three stoplights. At the moment, the largest nearby store was a Walmart, which lay fifteen minutes in the other direction. Local inhabitants regarded the influx of income that the Cuelebres brought the local economy with varying degrees of disconcertment and delight.

She grimaced. "Apparently some of the city would like to move upstate with us. Several people made a point of telling me that new shops and businesses were going to open up soon, including restaurants, clothing stores, a gourmet food store, a delicatessen and a more upscale hotel."

He frowned. "Some of that will be good, but we don't want it to get out of hand, or we could lose the reasons why we wanted to move in the first place. I'll talk to the town trustees about ways to limit the expansion."

"I think that's a good idea." She glanced down at the top of Liam's head and said softly, "I'm going to tuck him into his crib."

Dragos nodded, his expression softening as he looked down at Liam too. "Now that you're back, I'll head out to the site. I want to see how much headway they've made in the blasting today."

"Okay." She smiled at him. "See you later."

He answered her smile with a slow, wicked one of his own. "But not too much later. I fancy an early bedtime tonight."

She watched him walk away, thinking happy, comfortable thoughts. Dinner then bed, and who knew when they would finally fall asleep? They could take their time tonight. They had all the time in the world.

Less than half an hour later, she would give anything to call him back to her again. Anything to keep him from walking away.

Oh gods, anything.

✧   ✧   ✧

SHE TOOK LIAM upstairs, to his bedroom in the right wing of the house.

The right wing held their master suite, which included a wide balcony, a massive bedroom, a sitting room decorated with simple, elegant cream-colored furniture, a giant plasma television and a glass-fronted fireplace with a beautiful, streamlined slate mantle set against floor-to-ceiling windows that faced the Adirondack Mountains. They also had walk-in closets and a bathroom that rivaled the one in their New York penthouse for size and luxury.

Liam's nursery lay adjacent to their suite and included his bedroom, a bath, and a playroom with a small kitchenette set in one corner so that snacks could be made quickly and easily for the growing boy, and everything was decorated in bright, happy colors. Other bedrooms in the wing were available for Liam's caretakers whenever they were on duty watching him.

The left wing held the guest rooms, while downstairs there was a large library with an office nook for Pia, a massive, state-of-the-art office for Dragos, a formal receiving room, the more private, informal sunroom that led to the back patio area, the kitchen and breakfast dining area, and a dining room that seemed, at least to her, to be half the size of a football field.

The lower level held a giant recreation room with TVs, a pool table, and a wet bar that any New York restaurant would be proud to own. Also included below were an extensive wine cellar and a long-term larder, and security specialists had installed a panic room known only to Dragos, Pia, the sentinels, and Pia's bodyguards.

Sometimes Pia felt like she needed a GPS just to get around the place. Still, she reminded herself, the house was in no way as huge or complex as Cuelebre Tower in New York, and despite the construction, in some ways it already felt more intimate. She could see glimpses of the beautiful home it was becoming, filled with her favorite colors and hand-picked pieces of furniture, and she loved the personal spaces they had created for themselves and for Liam.

When she entered Liam's bedroom, he didn't even stir as she kissed his forehead lightly and eased him into his crib. As always when he slept, he had turned into a little furnace, and she was grateful to get some fresh air against her skin after she put him down.

She turned on his baby monitor and went into their suite to shower and change into a knee-length, lime green and yellow summer dress, along with flat sandals. Her new haircut and pretty outfit made her happy, and she hummed underneath her breath as she stroked on some eye shadow and lip gloss.

A knock sounded on the suite door. When she called out an invitation, Eva opened the door and sauntered in.

The other woman's dark brown skin and bold features were accentuated by a saucy red, bustier-style top and jeans, and while she was armed—she always went armed—she looked as relaxed as Pia had ever seen her.

"Just wanted to know what was up for the rest of the day," Eva said. "You want to go out again?"

She shook her head. "Nope, we're going to stay in toni—"

As she spoke, another low boom like thunder rolled through the air.

A lightning bolt of pain struck her in the head. Her vision whited out. Dimly, she felt the container of lip gloss slide from lax fingers as she staggered and fell in an ungainly sprawl. More pain flared as she struck her knee against the corner of a nearby dresser.

Almost immediately, her vision cleared and the pain in her head eased, leaving behind a sense of dread so strong, it came in a wave of nausea.

Swearing, Eva dropped to her knees beside Pia and gathered her up in strong arms. "What the righteous fuck—Pia, talk to me. What's the matter?"

After the wave of dread came panic.

Pia had experienced that kind of panic before. It was the kind you felt when you were staring at the end of your life.

And she knew. She knew.

Shoving Eva away, she scrambled to her feet. "Something's wrong." Her voice shook. It was something bad. Killing bad. "Something happened to Dragos. Watch Liam. Don't leave him."

Almost as quickly, Eva sprang upright too. As she switched to bodyguard mode, her expression changed and became deadly.

She made the mistake of taking hold of Pia's arm. "Stay here until we can find out what happened. You can't go running into an unknown situation. It could be dangerous."

The panic rode Pia harder than any devil could have, and she rounded on Eva with a wild animal's ferocity. "Oh, can't I? You fucking watch me. *Stay here and guard my son.*"

Eva's eyes widened. Her grip loosened, and she fell back a step.

Pia had nothing more to say. She had used up her words, all but one. The wild animal that had taken over her body whirled and sprinted down the hall. She flew down the stairs, burst out of the house and raced down the path to the construction site. She had never run so fast in her life.

As fast as she ran, it wasn't fast enough to stop what had happened to her mate, and the only word she had left inside of her was his name.

Dragos.

Chapter Two

BURSTING OUT OF the tree line, she reached the construction site bordering the lake.

The scene looked strange and wrong. It took her a few heartbeats to realize why.

The dimensions of the clearing had changed. A section of bedrock had collapsed, and at the pile of rubble at the base of a bluff, people swirled in a melee of urgency, the yellow of their hard hats bobbing through a growing haze of dust.

Others stared, their expressions aghast. She grabbed the nearest worker by the front of his shirt. "Where is he?"

He didn't ask whom she meant. Wordlessly, he pointed at the rubble.

Letting go of him, she raced toward the group who were digging frantically at the pile of rubble and shifting the heavier rocks. Leaping over obstacles, she landed beside the man shouting directions at the rest of the crew. He caught sight of her and fell silent, abruptly, and the expression in his gaze carried the same weight of horror as everyone else on the scene.

"Tell me he's not here," she said between her teeth.

Snatching off his hard hat, he shoved it onto her head. "He's here, along with the shift foreman and another man."

She had already known it, but still, the stark words struck her like a punch to the stomach. Blindly, she turned toward the rubble and started to dig like the others, bare-handed in case a vulnerable body lay close underneath the surface.

He had to be okay. He had to. Even in his human form, he was unbelievably strong.

Last year, when they had been in a car wreck— before they had really mated—he had *pushed* out with his Power to keep the car from crushing them. He could bend metal with his bare hands. He...

He had always said he'd seen the car wreck coming, and he'd been able to brace himself. What if he hadn't seen this coming?

She only became aware she was sobbing under her breath when strong, dark hands came down on her shoulders.

"Hugh's watching Liam," Eva said in her ear. "I couldn't leave you to come out here on your own."

She glanced over her shoulder, took in Eva's sober, compassionate expression and her snarl died in her throat. Blinking rapidly, she nodded.

Eva glanced down at Pia's hands, which were scraped and bleeding. "I'll find you some gloves."

Not bothering to answer, Pia turned back to the rubble and started digging again.

"I found Jake!" a man shouted, to her left.

Instantly the focus of attention shifted, and several men converged together to quickly dig out the unmoving man. At some point EMTs had arrived. Pia saw uniformed paramedics racing to the spot carrying a stretcher and medical bags.

As they lifted the man's limp body onto the stretcher, she looked away. Maybe she should care that they had found someone alive, but she didn't. Maybe she could care later. All she cared about right now was that they hadn't found Dragos yet.

He couldn't be dead. Just the thought of it made her world stop, and she had to struggle to breathe.

Come on, she said telepathically. *Where are you? COME ON!*

The pile of rubble exploded.

Dragos's mountainous dragon form appeared in front of her, his iridescent bronze hide dulled in a coating of dust. The sheer size of his body knocked aside rocks, equipment and men alike.

Something hit her in the chest, and she tumbled backward. Ignoring the hail of debris that fell on her, she climbed to her feet, joy and relief bringing tears to her eyes.

Oh, thank God, she told him. *I've been so scared....*

The bronze dragon's immense, triangular head swept from side to side as glaring gold eyes took in the surrounding scene.

As he did so, hot, wet droplets of moisture splattered her in the face and chest.

It was blood. Her gaze focused on a jagged gash that

ran along the dragon's brow. Bright liquid crimson streamed down the long arch of his neck.

It's okay, she said to him. While virtually everyone else scrambled to get out of his way, she climbed over the rocks toward him, hand outstretched. *I'm here. You're going to be okay….*

The dragon mantled gigantic wings, strewing more debris and throwing a shadow over the clearing. Snapping his head back around to her, he bared wicked, razor-sharp teeth as long as her torso.

Face upturned, she stood motionless as his massive, monstrous head snaked toward her.

The dragon's jaws opened wide, and *he snapped at her.*

Hot breath blasted her hair back from her face. The edge of the dragon's teeth tore through the front of her dress, and Eva slammed into her from the side, tackling her to the ground.

It knocked the breath out of her. Even as she coughed and struggled to take a wheezing breath, her gaze never left Dragos as all her emotions and beliefs vaporized. Like the collapsing bedrock, they crumbled to dust.

All the terror and dread of the last several minutes, and all the joy and relief.

The unshakeable foundation of her faith that he would never, could never, hurt her.

Tail lashing from side to side, the dragon roared. The gigantic sound shook the earth, and fire boiled out of his massive, parted jaws. Spraying fire in a circle, he sent people screaming as they ran away.

His wings hammered down, and he launched.

As she watched the dragon climb in the air, wheel and wing away, she didn't know she could exist in such a cold, barren place.

She watched him until he had shrunk to a small speck in the sky and disappeared.

Come back, she whispered. *Come back.*

But her whisper was small and uncertain.

A million miles away, Eva rolled off her body and yanked her up by the shoulders. The other woman seemed to be shouting at her. She focused on Eva's lips as they shaped words. Are you hurt? Did you get burned anywhere?

One side of Eva's face was blistered, her dark eyes wide.

Pia looked around the clearing. Other people were burned and stumbling to help each other, some standing still as they stared up at the empty sky. Glancing down at herself, she fingered her dress. The bright material was torn, sheared by the edge of the dragon's teeth.

The immense distance between her and the rest of the world started to dissipate, and pain intruded. Her chest hurt, and her legs and back felt scraped and bruised from landing in a sprawl on the rocky, uneven ground.

Her ability to think returned as well, but thankfully all her emotions stayed away. Glancing down at her scraped, raw fingers, she laid her hand gently against Eva's burned cheek and watched as the other woman's burns faded away.

She said, "I need a phone. Now."

Eva nodded and whirled away. When she returned a few moments later, she held out a cell phone wordlessly.

Taking it, Pia dialed a number she knew by heart and listened to ringing.

A moment later, the call was answered.

Graydon said, "I don't know this number. Who are you?"

"Gray," she said. "I need you."

"Pia? Is that you, cupcake?"

In her mind's eye, she saw again the dragon's teeth approaching.

Snapping at her.

"I need all the sentinels," she told him. Her shoulders shuddered, as if her body wanted to sob again. She shut that down hard. She didn't have time to cry. "You'd better bring the demesne lawyers with you."

His voice sharpened, all the mild good humor falling away. "What happened? Where's Dragos?"

She lifted her head and stared at the empty sky. "We're not talking about it over the phone," she said softly. "But I think you should bring some treasure too. Lots and lots of treasure."

ONE SMALL BLESSING had occurred.

Everyone had already been scrambling to get away from Dragos, so the dragon's fire had caused only light burns. There was only one casualty from the construction site accident—Ned Brandling, the shift foreman.

Back at the house, Eva told her about Brandling's

death while she took another quick shower to wash away the dust and grime. The scrapes on her fingers had already healed, and the bruises along her back and legs were fading.

Neither of them had mentioned Dragos's name since he had disappeared. Pia could tell by the quick, nervous way Eva spoke that the other woman was scared, but she had nothing to offer as reassurance or comfort.

After her shower, she dressed in sturdy clothes, knee-length jean shorts and a T-shirt, and tennis shoes. She moved fast, because she could hear Liam crying over the baby monitor, along with Hugh's gentle attempts to comfort him.

As soon as she had yanked on her shoes, Eva straightened. "What now?"

Pia said, "I'm going to take care of Liam. Go clean up."

Scowling, Eva flexed her hands. "I'm not leaving you."

The other woman was still covered in dust from the site. Pia glanced at her and shook her head. "You're not going into Liam's nursery like that. God only knows what he can sense of what's happened, and he already sounds frightened enough as it is. I don't want you upsetting him any further."

Looking abashed, Eva ducked her head. "Sorry," she muttered. "I didn't think. I'll get cleaned up and be right back."

Without further delay, Pia went into Liam's nursery. Hugh was cradling and walking him. As soon as Liam saw her, he wailed louder and tried to throw his body forward, reaching for her.

A sharp sliver of feeling wormed its way into her frozen heart. Gathering Liam close, she walked over to the rocking chair and pulled his favorite blanket around him.

Looking up into Hugh's worried expression, she said, "See that we're not disturbed until the sentinels arrive."

"Yes, ma'am," he said, his voice soft and careful. "I'll keep watch outside the door."

"Thank you."

As he eased the door shut behind him, she turned her attention to Liam. The toddler had clenched both fists into the front of her T-shirt. As soon as her eyes met his, his small face crumpled. The sliver of feeling in her heart grew larger until it was a hot, agonized pain, and she fought back tears of her own.

"Shh, my sweetest darling," she whispered, stroking Liam's silken head.

He put his cheek against hers in a gesture at once so mature and loving, it broke the tension in her spine, and she wrapped around him tightly. He clung to her, and neither of them moved until the door opened some time later, and Graydon strode in.

Graydon was the biggest of the sentinels, a burly, mild mannered giant almost as large as Dragos in his human form.

Just like Dragos, as always when Graydon entered the room, the available space seemed to shrink, due as much to the potent force of his personality as to his size.

He wore the sentinel's usual outfit of black T-shirt, jeans and boots—clothing that was sturdy enough for a rough, often violent lifestyle and easy to discard when damaged—along with a Glock in a holster clipped to the waist of his jeans.

As soon as he saw her and Liam in the rocking chair, he strode toward them, went down on one knee and would have taken them into his arms if she hadn't stopped him with one hand pressed against his chest.

She couldn't bear to be hugged at the moment, or she might break down. And she didn't have time to break down. She had too much to do.

One look into Graydon's darkened, sober gaze, and she could tell that he had already heard at least some version of what had happened.

She patted him on the chest in silent apology for rebuffing his hug, and he took her hand. He told her telepathically. *Everyone else is downstairs, except for Alex, who drew the short straw, and Aryal, who went down to the construction site to try to find out how the accident occurred.*

Unsurprised, she nodded. Whenever a situation was serious enough to call for the full strength of the sentinels, they always left one of them behind in New York to handle whatever might arise while the rest were gone.

The lawyers are here too?

His jaw tightened as he nodded. *Them too. And I wasn't sure what you meant by treasure, but I brought rough, uncut jewels and gold.*

That's fine, she said.

His rugged, weather-beaten face looked tight with

worry. *What do you need right now?*

Steeling her spine, she told him, *I need for the sentinels to find out where Dragos has gone. Just track him down. It's important you keep your presence cloaked. Don't approach him, and don't try to talk to him. He took a blow to the head. He was bleeding profusely, and—and—Graydon, he's not himself right now.*

His hand tightened on hers. *What do you mean? The stories we heard have been pretty confused. What really happened out there?*

Cupping the back of Liam's head, she met his gaze. *I mean the only reason he didn't kill me earlier was because Eva knocked me out of the way.*

His eyes dilated in a quick reaction to her words. *That's impossible. He would die before he ever hurt you.*

Of course he would, she snapped. Her mouth worked as she fought to keep her face from crumpling as Liam's had earlier. *If he remembered me, he would.*

Graydon's indrawn breath was sharp and audible. *Okay, we'll find him. I swear it.*

Do it fast, she said tightly. *There's only so much I can heal. When Quentin and Aryal were so badly injured in the spring, I could help them, but only to a certain extent. Too much time had passed, and they both ended up scarred.*

Also, much of her Wyr nature still remained a mystery to her. She had no idea if the healing properties in her blood would help Dragos's mental state, or if she could only heal physical wounds.

That was assuming she could coax the dragon into letting her close enough to heal him. If Dragos had suffered some kind of traumatic amnesia, there was a possibility he might never recover his memories.

And he had snapped at her.

Snapped.

Closing her eyes, she tightened her jaw against the memory.

Wyr mated for life, but nobody fully understood why. It was a complicated process involving emotions, sexual attraction, timing and opportunity.

What if Dragos couldn't remember that he was Lord of the Wyr? That she was his mate? What if he *never* remembered? Could he live as though he had never mated before?

The thought made her feel physically ill. Maybe he could. Maybe… theoretically, he could even fall in love and mate with someone else, but if that happened, where would that leave her?

That was the panic talking. Forcing herself to breathe evenly, she backed away from the hectic questions hurtling through her mind.

We won't rest until we locate him, Graydon told her. He clenched her hand so hard, her fingers ached. *If he's that badly injured, he won't have flown far.*

I hope you're right, she muttered.

As they fell silent, she pressed her lips against Liam's forehead. If Dragos was her heart, this precious boy was her soul. She would do everything in her power to safeguard him, but she couldn't protect him from what was happening to them now.

Keeping her voice calm and gentle, she said, "Peanut,

my love, you have to be a big soldier now."

Lifting his head from her shoulder, Liam looked at her with absolute trust in his eyes, and she thought, I cannot believe I am saying these horrible words to that small, sweet face. Swallowing the thought, she smiled at him. As he tried to smile back, the crazed animal inside of her wanted to howl and rip down the walls of the house.

Stroking Liam's cheek, she told him, "You need to be good for Hugh and Eva, while I need to talk to some lawyers about some boring legal stuff."

Boring things like power of attorney, and line of Wyr succession. Sorting out the legalities of inheritance had been high on their to-do list, but they had been so busy since Liam had been born in the spring, they hadn't yet gotten to it, and immortality had a sneaky way of lulling one into a false sense of security.

If the absolute worst came to worst, Graydon would make an outstanding father and a steady regent in the Wyr demesne until Liam came of age.

But she had no intention of letting the worst happen.

"After I finish dealing with all of that," she told Liam softly, "I'm going to go get Daddy back."

Chapter Three

THE DRAGON HAD a splitting headache, so he didn't fly down immediately to kill the fool who approached from below. Instead he stretched out along a shelf of rock near the top of a low mountain and basked in the afternoon sunshine while he waited for the fool to hike to him.

After all, he could always slaughter the fool with a minimum of effort once she drew close enough.

He could tell she was female from the snatches of her scent that wafted toward him on the hot summer breeze.

He could tell she was a fool, because it had become clear some time ago that she climbed toward him, not by accident but with intent. She was a small, slender-looking creature, and alone, and he didn't think she was armed with any weapons. And really, he couldn't fathom why any lone person would approach him without weapons, so she had to be suicidal as well.

Her scent bothered him, and he shifted the bulk of his body restlessly as he drew in great breaths of air. Strange, feminine and evocative, it tugged at something deep inside. He could almost recall what kind of creature she was, almost grasp at a tantalizing something that lay just beyond his reach….

Each time he came close to it, the tantalizing something slipped away again.

She wasn't Elven. He hated the Elves with a passion born of long-ago, shadowy memories of war. No Elf would approach him for any good reason, and if she had been Elven, blazing headache or no, he would have flown down from his perch and torn her to shreds for daring to encroach upon his space.

Flexing his talons at the murderous thoughts, he crawled forward to lap thirstily at the bubbling spring of cold water that ran down the steep mountainside beside his ledge. The spring was one of the reasons why he had chosen this place to rest. In this remote spot, the dragon had water, sunlight and a high vantage point to watch for enemies. He could rest here until his headache eased and his vision improved enough so he could hunt for food.

Windswept clouds danced overhead in the bright, aquamarine sky. It would almost be peaceful, except for the pain in his head and the nearing fool.

Who wasn't Elven.

Who was, somehow, both like the dragon and yet dramatically unlike him at the same time.

As her scent grew nearer and stronger, it evoked images of cool, wild moonlight, a fantastic Power pouring over him like a benediction for the damned, and a sense of a unique treasure more precious than anything the dragon had ever seen before or comprehended.

So. That was more than reason enough to let the fool

live for the moment. The dragon's predatory thoughts wound like a serpent coiling on itself.

He would let her get close enough so he could discover for himself what kind of creature she was, but most importantly, so he could find out where she had hidden that fantastic, unique treasure and claim it for himself.

Still, the pain made him cranky and inclined to be vicious.

It was a good thing for her continued health and well-being that she approached him slowly, making a certain amount of polite noise—not too loud, but enough that they were both fully aware that they knew of each other's existence.

He waited until she reached the edge of the clearing surrounding his ledge. When he heard the sound of a small rock shifting underneath one of her shoes, the dragon said, "That's close enough."

Dead silence, as she froze.

The dragon lifted his head and glared at the fool out of his one good eye. She wasn't Elven, and although she looked human enough, she wasn't human either.

Like, yet unlike him in some fundamental way.

She was suntanned and slender, with long, bare legs, and she carried a heavy-looking, sturdy pack on her back. Her hair was the color of sunshine, the color of precious gold, and her eyes... he hadn't been prepared for the impact of her large, wary eyes. They were a beautiful rich, dark violet, and they embodied the very essence of cool, wild moonlight.

Her eyes confused and agitated him.

The dragon growled, "You disturb me."

Ducking her golden head, the female averted her gaze. "I apologize."

She was soft-spoken, her voice gentle. He had dreamed of such a voice whispering to him brokenly through the night. *Come back. Come back to me.*

The memory of the dream made him shake his head. Pain flared at the movement, and he bared his teeth in defiance against it. "Why do you dare bother me, and why should I let you survive it?"

"I brought you gifts."

Gifts?

Nobody brought the dragon gifts. The very idea was laughable.

While there was fear in the female's expression as she spoke, she watched him steadily without backing away, and her fear was not gratifying to him.

In fact, her fear disturbed him in a deeply profound way. He couldn't think clearly enough to puzzle it out. Leaning his aching head against the side of a boulder, he snapped, "What kind of gifts?"

"I would be glad to show you," she said in her soft, gentle voice. "But I'm afraid you might not be able to see them properly. It looks like you have dried blood in one of your eyes."

As soon as she said it, he realized it was true. Raising one forepaw, he rubbed at the eye on his blind side, which made the pain worse.

"Perhaps you might be able to see better if you could

rinse some of the blood away," the female suggested. "I would be glad to help you, if you like."

Snapping his head up, he hissed, "Stay back."

She recoiled, the fear flaring again in her wide gaze. "Of course. I only meant to help."

The dragon could hear the truth in her voice, and once again, her fear disturbed him at some deep level. He growled, "Stay exactly where you are. I will deal with this myself."

"Yes, all right," she whispered.

He shifted closer to the spring, and, craning his neck, he managed to angle the injured side of his head under running water. The icy wetness cascaded over his hide, washing away the blood. It also helped to ease the pain somewhat, and he heaved a sigh of relief.

He stayed like that for some time, until his thoughts came with more clarity, and he was able to work his eye open. Lifting his head, he shook off the water and turned back to the female.

She had eased the pack from her back and taken a seat on the ground, resting her bright head in her hands. Her posture was at once both weary and so dejected, the sight tugged at him.

Troubled by his mysterious reactions to her, his crankiness returned. He hadn't asked for her to climb up his mountain and inflict her unwanted presence or emotions on him. "Now," the dragon said in a silken tone of voice, "what is this nonsense about you bringing me gifts?"

Her head came up. "I did. Can I show them to you

now?"

Enjoying the way her hair glinted in the sunlight, he relaxed back against the hot stone ledge. The only reason why she would have brought him anything was because she wanted something from him. The more value there was in her gift, the more she would want from him. There was something wily about this female, and he meant to get to the bottom of why she had come.

"Very well," he told her.

He watched her from under lowered eyelids, as she opened her pack and drew out cloth-wrapped packages tied with twine. Taking the largest and clearly the heaviest, she set it on the ground, untied the twine and pulled back the cloth to reveal several bricks made of gold.

While he didn't abandon his relaxed posture, inside the dragon grew tense. Valuable gifts, indeed. He said, "Show me the rest."

She appeared eager now, as she did as he ordered. The next package she bared for his sharp gaze was much smaller and contained a handful of clear, shining rocks that reflected shards of light as icy as the mountain spring. Diamonds. The third package she opened held stones of such rich, deep violet-hued blue they had to be sapphires.

For a long moment, the dragon looked at the rich array of offerings spread on the ground. He could tell by the bulk of her pack that it wasn't empty, but what she had offered him was more than enough. Gold, diamonds and sapphires, all of which he loved. She had brought his favorite things.

When at last he looked up, his gaze had turned cold and deadly. "Who are you, and what do you want?"

At one side of her tense mouth, a delicate muscle flexed. Taking a deep breath, she said with quiet deliberation, "My name is Pia Cuelebre. What's yours?"

Cuelebre.

He knew that name. It meant winged serpent.

As soon as she said it, hot agony flared in his head again. There was a well of knowledge that lay just on the other side of that wall of fiery pain, something vital to his existence, but he couldn't access it.

He could access her, though.

Shock flared across her face as he lunged at her and pinned her to the ground underneath one outspread forepaw. She was so fragile he could crush her with a shrug.

So fragile.

She had climbed all this way to confront him, and she lay without weaponry or defenses of any kind. Not even her cool mysterious Power had flared to strike back at him. He held the bulk of his body tense, as he stared down at her in confusion. Gripping his talons on either side of her slender neck, she stared back unwaveringly at him, her body trembling.

He hissed, "You are no winged serpent."

"No, I'm not," she whispered. "But that's still my name. What's your name—or do you have one?"

The dragon had a name. He had chosen it for himself. He reached for it and ran into that wall of fiery pain again.

The female's gaze darkened and filled with moisture. One droplet slipped out the corner of her eye and streaked down her temple. "You don't know, do you?"

"Be silent," he ordered. Serpentine coils of thought writhing, he struggled to reach past the fiery wall in his head.

Agony drove him back, defeating him.

A hint of calculation flashed across her expression. She said, "I have another gift for you."

He bared his teeth. He didn't trust her gifts. "What?"

"Knowledge," she told him.

Carefully, he dug the tips of his talons into the ground around her prone body. Carefully, so that his threat was clear while he didn't hurt her. Not yet. He reserved that possibility for later.

"Why do you think your knowledge is of any use to me?" He let the possibility of her death darken his voice.

She swallowed. "Answer two questions, and I'll try to show you."

He paused suspiciously, suspecting a trick, but she could only trick him if he chose to answer. In the meantime, he might learn something valuable in the nature of her questions. "Ask."

The breath shook audibly in her throat. She whispered, "How many nights have you spent on this mountain?"

His gaze narrowed. If there was some kind of trick in such a simple question, he couldn't see what it was. "One. And your next question?"

"Where were you yesterday morning?"

Even as he tried to think back to the answer, he slammed into the fiery wall. His vision glazed. Rearing away from her, the dragon released his frustration and pain in a bellow of rage aimed at the sky.

When he could focus again, he discovered she had scrambled to the tree line at the edge of the clearing and crouched with her back pressed against the trunk of a tree.

Frankly, he was astonished she hadn't taken off running down the mountain, and he glanced back down at the array of gold and jewels at his feet. "What do you want from me in return for all of this, along with your precious knowledge?"

She scrubbed her face with the back of one hand, leaving a smear of dirt behind. Her voice shook as she told him, "You're the only one who can help me find my mate again."

Drawing in a deep breath, the dragon let her scent fill his lungs, and he realized something that had lain in the back of his mind for some time.

Like, but unlike.

He didn't know what kind of creature she was, but she was no predator. If she had been, he really might have killed her once she had dared to reach his ledge.

He realized something else, as disjointed images ran through his mind.

An explosion of pain, the first pain. Crushing weight and darkness. Shouting from a distance.

And a voice in the darkness. *Her* voice?

Where are you? COME ON!

"Yesterday," he said. "You were one of the people who attacked me."

Dismay bolted across her features, and she straightened with a jerk. "No—that's not what happened!"

The dragon regarded her cynically. Wyrm, he was called. The Great Beast. Traps had been laid for him before, and he had been attacked, but no one had ever brought him down. "It wasn't? Then what would you call it?"

Rubbing her forehead with both hands, she said tightly, "I would call it a horrific misunderstanding." She dropped her hands and looked at him, and either anger or desperation flashed in her eyes. Or maybe both. "If you can recall anything at all about yesterday, try to think back to what I said to you. I said, 'It's okay. You're going to be okay.' Do you remember that?"

He tilted his head, eyes narrowing. He had no recollection of what she said, only the voice in the darkness, but once again, there was no hint of a lie in her voice.

He said, "No."

Her shoulders sagged. "I know your name," she told him. "Your name is Dragos."

A thread of recognition ran through him, like a jolt of electricity.

Dragos.

Yes, that was his name, but the rest of what she said... he strained to think back.

The female—she said her name was Pia—was continuing, her words tumbling rapidly over each other as she stepped forward. "You're obviously in pain. I don't think you realize how seriously you're hurt, but if you will only let me look at your wound, I swear I can help you."

She pushed him too hard, too far. The only things he could recall were the pain, being buried under a heavy weight, a heavy cloud of dust covering the scene like a shroud and people shouting.

"Stop," Dragos said. "I'm done talking. I need to think."

Alarm filled her expression. "No, you have to listen to me. This is more important than you can possibly understand—"

"Enough." He growled it with such intensity, the ground behind them vibrated. "I have listened to you enough. I have never needed healing from anyone before, and I will not tolerate you trying to convince me that I need it now."

She stared at him in astonishment and the beginnings of bitterness. "That's not true," she said, her voice clipped. "You've needed my healing before. You just don't remember it."

"If I don't remember it," the dragon said, "how can I trust you're telling the truth?" He spread out one fore-paw to indicate the gold and jewels. "You bring me convenient gifts of all my favorite things. Do you think I've never seen a trap baited with such as this before?"

She stared at him, breathing heavily, but remained silent. Then her chin came up. "Fine. Maybe bringing the treasure was a mistake, but I'm not leaving."

"As you wish," Dragos said.

He glanced dismissively once more at the treasure lying on the ground between them, then turned his back on her, gathered himself and sprang into flight.

The last thing he wanted to do was go hunting, but he needed food to heal and time to think. Either the female would be waiting for him when he returned, or she would not. If she truly wanted to find her mate again, she would wait.

If he returned.

Chapter Four

PIA STARED UP at the sky, watching Dragos leave. Normally she loved to see him take flight, but now watching the dragon fly away gave her a sick feeling in the pit of her stomach. How far would he go?

How could she be so stupid?

The satellite phone in her pack rang, and she dug it out to answer it.

Graydon demanded, "Are you all right? He didn't hurt you did he?"

She looked in the direction of the low, nearby peak of a neighboring mountain, where the gryphon hid, keeping watch from a distance. It said something, didn't it, that Graydon would even ask such a thing. A week ago—a day ago—the question would have been unthinkable.

"No," she said dully. "He didn't hurt me." At least, he hadn't hurt her anywhere that was visible. Inside, she felt like she was slowly bleeding from some vital artery.

"I'll follow him."

"No! Leave him be for now." Unable to stand still, she paced through the clearing. "It's my fault he left. I panicked and pushed him too hard. The gold and jewels—they were a bad idea. He doesn't remember me. He doesn't remember, Gray, and of course he was suspicious. I'd brought all his favorite things, and he thought I was baiting some kind of trap."

"Take a deep breath," Graydon said gently. "You didn't do anything wrong. It was a good idea, as far as it went. Are you sure I shouldn't track him? What if he doesn't come back?"

Scrubbing at her face with the back of one hand, she tried to think. Where would he go? What would he do?

She was excellent at predicting what Dragos would do and where he would go, but she had no idea what this strange, frightening creature might decide. The thought of the dragon prowling unchecked through the countryside made her stomach tighten even further.

But she had roused the dragon's suspicions, and if he sensed Graydon following him, Dragos might attack him. Graydon could get hurt, or worse, killed. Dragos would never forgive himself if that happened, and she would never forgive herself either. Graydon's kind, steady presence was one of the reasons why she had made it through such a dark, awful night, and she couldn't bear the thought of losing him.

"No," she said again. "We can't risk it. Maybe I raised enough questions in his mind that he'll come back on his own for answers. He said he needed to think. For the moment, we're going to have to trust him, and wait to see if he returns on his own."

Those were some of the toughest words she'd ever had to say. They ranked right up there with telling Liam *you have to be a big soldier now.* The panicked animal inside her wanted nothing more than to chase after Dragos, but the thought of trusting the dragon who was even now acting without Dragos's memories was almost insupportable.

"I want to join you," Graydon said. "It's going against all my instincts to leave you there alone."

"Well, you can't," she replied flatly. "If he comes back, and he smells your scent, he'll be even more convinced this is some kind of trap." She glanced once more up into the sky. "For now, we'll just have to wait."

"Call me if anything changes, or if you need me to come. In fact, call me every half hour," Graydon said. "I want to hear the sound of your voice, and know you're okay."

She knew what he wanted. Like Eva, he was scared, and he wanted reassurance. With the fact that Wyr mated for life, and with Dragos so critically injured, everything about their lives was unpredictable now, unstable.

But she had no more reassurance to offer Graydon than she'd had to offer Eva.

She said, "I'm not going to pretend to be fine. To tell you the truth, I feel pretty crazy, and I feel like I'm fighting for my life. But you're going to have to trust me, too. I'm dealing with it. I'll deal. And I'll call you if I need you."

He swore under his breath. After a moment, he said, "Okay, sweetheart."

Hanging up, she stuffed the phone back into one of the side pockets of the pack. She had to get her act together. She didn't know how long Dragos would be gone, and she was exhausted. Waiting through the long, terrible night as the sentinels searched for Dragos, dealing with legalities for both the Wyr demesne and for Liam's sake—just in case—and the long hike up the mountain, along with confronting the dragon, had all taken their toll.

She needed to refuel and rest, at least as much as she was able, because she had no idea what would happen next.

Moving to the spring, she washed her face and arms in the icy water then drank as much as she could hold. Afterward, she forced herself to choke down a couple of vegan protein bars, and she wrapped up the gold bricks and jewels and stuffed them back into her pack.

The heat of the afternoon was fading, and the shadows from the trees lengthened. Even though it was high summer, it got cold in the mountains at night. She pulled one of the last treasures from her pack, a sturdy, flannel-lined jacket. Wrapping it around her torso, she curled into a tight ball against the trunk of the tree and fell into an uneasy doze.

Come back. Please come back to me.

✦   ✦   ✦

THE RUSH OF gigantic wings roused her.

Scrambling to her feet, she watched as the dragon wheeled overhead. Inside, relief and tension grappled for supremacy, but in the end relief won out.

He had returned, and he didn't have to. He could

have just as easily left. He had no stake in this location. He came back because she was here, and he wanted those answers.

While she had dozed, afternoon had turned to early evening, and the sky overhead had turned vivid, framing the dragon's bronze body with jewel tones. Light and graceful as a cat, despite his massive size, he landed on the ledge.

His muzzle was coated with bright, fresh blood. She could smell it from where she stood. It was cow's blood. Somewhere nearby, a farmer was missing some cattle. If we survive this, she thought with grim gallows humor, someone is going to have to hunt that farmer down and pay him for his trouble.

Ignoring her as if she didn't exist, Dragos strode to the spring to rinse his muzzle and forepaws, sleek muscle flowing under his bronze hide.

She studied him thoughtfully. He seemed to be moving better, with more ease and surety. The jagged wound at his brow looked partially healed, but she didn't know whether to be relieved or worried about that.

All she knew was that she wasn't buying his act. He might pretend to ignore her but he knew very well, probably to a fraction of an inch, where she was standing.

Still without looking at her, Dragos said, "Where's my treasure?"

His treasure. She cocked her head, resting her hands on her hips. If the situation hadn't been so serious she might have smiled. Even now, amidst all his suspicions, the dragon remained as possessive as ever.

"I apologize for what happened earlier," she said, keeping her voice as soft and even as she had before. Nonaggressive, nonthreatening. "I understand that you have cause to be suspicious of anyone who approaches you as I did, but I meant no insult by offering the gifts, nor was I baiting any kind of trap. I was only hoping to strike a bargain with you."

"Ah, yes," he replied, glancing cynically over his shoulder. "Because I'm the only one who can help you find your mate."

She hesitated. "Yes."

He finished washing, circled and stretched out on the rough, stony ledge with all the arrogance of an emperor assuming his throne. Only then did he look directly at her, the expression in his great, gold eyes confrontational and cold.

The impact was almost overwhelming. She had seen him give his enemies just such a look before, but he had never looked that way at her until now.

He said, "That doesn't answer my question."

Tucking in her chin, she leveled her gaze at him. While he might have chosen to return, the decision seemed to have put him in a pissy mood. "What difference does it make? You clearly didn't want it."

The dragon narrowed his eyes. "I've changed my mind. You will bring it to me."

Normally, her impulse would be to back talk to all that monumental arrogance, but she curbed it. Now wasn't the time to sass him. There was no hint of indulgence in his current demeanor, or softness. This was all about establishing dominance. His entire attitude demanded that she prove herself.

Bowing her head, she knelt to open her pack and pull out the packets of gold and jewels. Gathering them in her arms, she walked toward him. About fifteen feet away, she slowed to a stop. When she made as if to kneel, Dragos said, "Bring it closer."

Obediently, she took a few steps closer. The force of his personality pressed against her skin. His Power boiled around his physical form like an invisible corona, and despite the gravity of the situation, the desperate animal inside of her drew comfort from his closeness and calmed.

"Closer," the dragon said again, watching her intently.

He was lethally unpredictable, easily the most dangerous creature she had ever known or met, and at the moment, he did not remember he loved her.

She was supposed to stay wary of him, but it was too hard to maintain when she was so tired and it went against every one of her instincts. With a sigh, she approached until she could set the packets on the ground between his outstretched forelegs.

When she straightened, he lowered his head until the large curve of his nostrils stopped a few inches from her hair. They stood like that for some time, breathing quietly. As she looked up into one immense, molten eye, she wanted very badly to stroke his muzzle, or to take out her small penknife, slice the palm of her hand and lay it against that terrible, half-healed wound on his brow.

That wound had taken everything from her. No matter how suspiciously or aggressively Dragos treated her at the moment, she never forgot—that wound was the real enemy.

But she didn't dare go quite that far, not without his express permission. If she made a mistake and pushed him too far, he could lash out at her again, and they would both lose everything.

"Now, tell me about this 'horrible misunderstanding,'" he ordered.

At a loss, she glanced around the clearing. How could she explain what had happened in such a way that the dragon could accept it? So much depended on concepts and relationships built over centuries.

He was Lord of the Wyr demesne, the head of a multibillion-dollar corporation, and a husband, mate and father, and yet earlier, the dragon didn't even know his own name.

Taking in a deep breath, she said in a cautious, low voice, "It wasn't any kind of attack. I swear it. You'll know that for yourself, as soon as you remember more."

"If it wasn't an attack, then what was it?"

"An accident," she whispered. She wiped her cheeks with both hands. "A terrible, terrible accident. You were helping with building a project, and you were all working together."

It was impossible to tell if he believed her. The dragon's face remained expressionless. "How did this accident occur?"

The evening before, she had asked the very same thing of Aryal, but she had only half comprehended the answer.

Now, she said, "I don't know all the details of what happened, but what I do know is that you were setting off a series of small, controlled explosions in a large section of bedrock that bordered a lake."

"Why?" He watched her closely.

"The site is where a large building is going to be constructed, so the area needs to be level in certain places. But there was a buried fault line in the rock nobody knew was there. It looked solid when it was inspected, but it wasn't. You—along with a couple of other men—you all thought you were safe where you were standing, around one edge of the bluff."

She paused, but he said nothing, his steady breathing stirring her hair. Lacing her fingers together, she twisted her hands and continued, "When the explosion went off, the force of it blew through the fault line, and blasted out where you were standing. They call that kind of accident 'flyrock' in construction and quarry blasting—it's material projected outside a declared danger zone. At least that's how it was explained to me. When the fault line was breached, a whole section of the area collapsed. You were all buried underneath it. One man died. The rest of you were badly injured."

After a moment, he said, "Your mate was at this building site."

The question took her by surprise, and she had to swallow before she could reply. "Yes," she whispered. "He's disappeared."

"You think I know where he is."

She shook her head. "No, but I believe you can help me find him."

"And you claim you've healed me before." The very lack of expression with which he said that indicated the depth of his skepticism.

"That must sound pretty outlandish to you." She tried to smile. "I guess it is pretty outlandish. It's been an outlandish kind of a year."

If he had such a hard time believing she might want to heal him, just wait until he found out about Peanut. She could imagine how well that conversation would go down.

"I don't remember you," he said.

Her head drooped. Of course, she knew that, but the clinical, dispassionate way in which he said it was every bit as devastating as the actual reality. All the passion she felt for him, this tremendous, consuming storm of love...

None of it was returned. None of the need, or his own love for her, manifested in anything he said or did. Here he was, as strong as ever, living and breathing in front of her, and she felt as if someone immeasurably precious to her had died.

"I wish, so very much, that I could find some way to convince you to let me heal you," she said unsteadily. "I wish it for your sake, so that you can feel better, and maybe—just maybe—your memories might return to you. But most of all, I wish it for my sake, because I miss my mate with all my heart, and I would do anything or give anything to get him back again."

"The wound is already healing." He added deliberately, "I don't need you either."

Maybe he was only speaking the truth as he knew it, but that seemed unnecessarily cruel, and it took everything she had not to lash out at him because of it.

Her voice hardened. "Maybe you don't need me, or maybe you only think you don't. You still don't remember what happened to you last week, or the week before, or the week before that. You don't know which of your old enemies might be close by, or what new enemies you might have made. You're vulnerable, Dragos, in a way you've never been vulnerable before, and I'm the only ally you've got who's offering you any kind of help."

Silence fell between them, and it was just long enough for her to castigate herself again for pushing him too hard when she had promised herself she wouldn't.

He stirred, shifting his long, bulky body, and by his very restlessness, she knew she had scored a hit.

"What is this healing you would attempt?" Dragos tilted his head to watch her more closely. "Do you really think it would help my memories return? I will not tolerate any kind of spell."

The surge of hope she felt was almost as unbearable as everything else had been in the last twenty-four hours.

"I can't tell you how much I hope it will help you get your memory back, but the truth is, I don't know," she told him. Unable to resist any longer, she laid a hand on his muzzle and stroked him. "I can promise you this—I would never hurt you."

A part of her thrilled to note he didn't pull back from her gentle caress, but then he had to go and spoil it.

"Of course you wouldn't, not if you have any hope of me helping you find your mate," he said, the cynical tone back in his voice.

She nearly smacked him on the nose, as she snapped, "Of course."

"Do it," he told her.

For a moment she could hardly believe her ears. Before he could change his mind, she dug into the front pocket of her jean shorts and pulled out her penknife. Under his sharp, distrustful gaze, she sliced open her palm.

"There's no spell," she told him, her voice tight with nerves. "It's just my blood. Bend your head to me."

Slowly, still watching her, the dragon bent his head down farther. She laid her bleeding palm lightly against his wound.

Power flowed out from her palm. Dragos sucked in a breath and shuddered. After a long moment, she pulled her hand away and inspected his wound in the failing light.

It had already been half healed, and as she watched, the wound faded into a bone white scar.

Dragos released a long sigh. She asked, "How do you feel?"

"Better. The headache is finally gone." The dragon met her gaze. "But I still don't remember you."

Chapter Five

A S HE SAID the words, Dragos watched the light that had brightened her eyes dim. Her eyes were quite beautiful, he realized. Large and expressive, they showed her every emotion. Her shoulders slumped, and her head bowed.

"Okay." Her voice had turned dull and flat, matching her dejected expression. "At least we tried."

She turned to walk away.

He frowned. He didn't like the sight of her walking away from him. The realization seemed to echo in his mind, almost as if he had thought it once before. "Where do you think you're going?"

"It's getting cold. I'm not like you. I don't have your kind of body heat. I'm going to gather wood for a fire." She didn't look around at him as she spoke. "I should have done it earlier."

His frown deepened. While his presence deterred other predators in the immediate area, the ground was rocky and steep, and the gathering dusk would make traversing it dangerous for someone who was so much more fragile than he.

He said abruptly, "I didn't say you could leave me."

Her stride hitched, and the angle of the back of her head seemed to express... exasperation? When she replied, her words had turned edged. "And I didn't ask you."

At that impudence, he growled a low warning, but she paid no attention and walked into the tree line. How dare she ignore him?

A new realization sidelined his burst of anger. While it was true he didn't remember her, the lack of pain and the absence of the fiery wall in his mind allowed something to surface—a single word that carried a huge concept.

Wyr.

Certainly she was unlike him, as she wasn't a predator, but still, she was like him in a fundamental way. They were both Wyr, both two-natured creatures.

Like him, she had an animal form that was somehow tied to her cool, witchy moonlit Power, the Power that had cascaded over his hot pain, easing and healing it.

And, like her, he had a human form.

Instinctively, he reached for his other form. It felt like flexing a familiar, well-toned muscle... and he shifted.

After the change, he regarded his body. In his human form, he was still much larger than she, taller and broader, and more heavily muscled. He was clad in jeans and a T-shirt, and sturdy boots, all of which were grimed with dirt and blood—his blood.

On his left hand, he wore a plain gold ring. As he stared at it curiously, he realized there was something attached to his wrist.

Holding up his hand, he inspected the thing on his wrist in the fading light.

It was a braid of gleaming, pale gold hair.

He sucked in a breath. No matter how suspiciously he might inspect the braid, the only touch of Power he felt on it was his own, and that felt like a protection spell. The braid of hair was just that, a simple braid.

And he had wanted to protect it.

The gold hair looked quite familiar. In fact, it looked like the exact shade of hair on the head of the woman who was even now stubbornly climbing around the steep mountainside in the growing dark.

Galvanized, he leaped after her. She had managed to travel much farther away from the clearing than he had expected. His gaze adjusting to the darker shadows under the trees, he tracked her by scent and instinct.

She crouched beside some deadfall, stacking sticks into the crook of one arm. As he approached, she pointed one stick toward him like a sword without looking up.

"Stay back," she said. Her voice sounded strange, clogged with emotion. "Leave me alone for a few minutes."

Distress seemed to bruise the air around her, and he could smell the tiny, telltale salt of tears. Scowling, Dragos folded his arms. He disliked the scent of her tears, and he had no intention of going anywhere just because she told him to.

"You're wasting your time," he told her abruptly.

"Those little twigs you're gathering will burn to ash within a half an hour."

She snapped, "It'll be better than nothing."

Brushing past the useless barrier of the stick she brandished and bending over her, he closed his hand carefully around the tense curve of her slender shoulder. She shuddered at his touch, her head tilting sideways as if she might lay her cheek against the back of his hand.

He waited for her to do it, and in the process discovered he savored the anticipation, but she didn't follow through with the gesture. Disappointment darkened his thoughts.

"Go back up to the clearing," he said. "I'll bring firewood."

Carefully, she pulled away from his touch and straightened. Still without looking at him, she told him stiltedly, "Thank you."

He lowered his head, watching her shadowed figure as she climbed back up to the ledge, still carrying her useless bundle of twigs. If he didn't like her walking away from him, he liked her pulling away from his touch even less.

They would have words about that. They would most definitely have words.

For now, he turned his attention back to the pile of deadfall. The frame of the fallen tree lay underneath a scatter of forest debris. With a few strong kicks, he splintered the dry wood and gathered several sturdy pieces. When he carried his load back to the clearing, he found that she had gathered rocks into a circle for a makeshift campfire ring.

Wordlessly, he stacked his load a few feet away from the ring, and went back for another load. When he returned and added the second armful to the stack, he found her squatting in front of the ring. She had stacked the sticks she had gathered, and she worked at lighting a handful of dry leaves with a small, handheld lighter.

Folding his arms, he watched. Even though he could have lit the fire with a single glance, she didn't ask for his help, and he didn't offer it. If she wanted to do it by herself, so be it.

After a few minutes, she had a small fire started. Tiny flames licked eagerly at the sticks, and the growing circle of light contrasted with the darkness around them.

Only then did she look up at him. She appeared calmer, more composed. She said, "It's a good sign that you remembered your human form. It's promising."

"Is it?" He tucked his chin and considered her from underneath lowered brows. "I suppose it is."

A powerful cascade of emotions made his mood uncertain, and apparently she picked up on it, for her gaze turned wary. "Don't you think so?"

The delicate skin around her eyes was shadowed with dark smudges, and she looked exhausted. Still, the firelight loved her, burnishing the warm, healthy tan of her skin. The pale gold of her hair shone.

Her hair.

He didn't look at his wrist.

"Perhaps it is a good sign," he conceded. "I find I have more questions as time goes on, thus more frustrations."

Feeding another stick to the fire, she nodded. In profile, her expression was grim, settled. She looked as though she were set upon a long journey requiring endurance.

Deciding to test her, he said, "I'm surprised you're still here. Once you realized I had no knowledge of your mate, I would have thought you'd have given up by now and left."

Anger flashed in her eyes, a deep, pure sapphire violet. The very best sapphires had that same intense, almost purple blue. "If you think I would give up searching for my mate, just because I've had a bad couple of days and a few setbacks, you're badly mistaken. I didn't mate for those times when it was convenient or easy for me—because, believe me, none of it has been convenient or easy. Not since the very first day."

The fire in her response was delicious. He wanted to bask in it, to eat it all up. And not once, since she had arrived, had she ever spoken a lie. Everything she had told him was the truth.

Still standing with his arms crossed, holding himself at a distance, he heard himself ask, "Tell me of this time before, when you claimed to have healed me."

There was a slight pause, as she adjusted to his change in focus. She lifted a shoulder. "I don't just claim to have healed you—I *have* healed you, three times now. The first time, last year, you were poisoned."

He didn't know what he had been expecting, but whatever it was, it certainly wasn't that. He drew in a breath between his teeth, on a slow hiss. "How?"

She paused, clearly searching for words. "It was a complicated situation, and I take a lot of responsibility for it. It was when we had first met, before we had grown to trust one another. Essentially, I provoked you into breaking some border treaties with the Elven demesne. They shot you with a poisoned arrow so that you couldn't shapeshift into the dragon while in their territory. You still have a scar on your chest where the arrow struck."

Reflexively, he rubbed the broad flat, muscled area of his right pectoral. Immediately, as if his fingers remembered more than he, they found a small indentation in the flesh. "And the second time?"

A dark expression shadowed her delicate, triangular face. "The second time you almost died. Again, the story is complicated, but basically you, along with some allies, fought a battle against an invader, one of the elder Elves who had come from a place called Numenlaur. You had several broken bones, and probably sustained other internal injuries. You couldn't defend yourself against the attacking army. Luckily, I was able to get to you in time."

The Elves again. Always, so many of his problems seemed to come down to the bloody Elves.

Going down on one knee, he added larger pieces of wood to the fire. The dry wood caught almost instantly, and the flames leaped higher, bringing light and heat to the cold night air.

"Now you've healed me again," he said. "It seems to have become something of a habit."

The shadow crossed across her expression again. "I wasn't able to heal you as much this time as I had hoped."

Lifting his head, he pinned her with his gaze. "What interesting stories you tell," he said softly. "But there is a notable lack of information in each one."

She lifted her chin. "Everything I've told you is true."

"I can tell that," Dragos said. "But what I want to know is, when were you going to tell me that I am your mate?"

Surprise visibly shook her, along with a resurgence of hope so palpable it was painful to witness. "You remembered?"

Earlier, when he'd looked at the gold ring he wore and the braided bracelet of hair, he had pieced the facts together. He was the destination, not part of her journey. He was the reason why she had climbed the mountain to face him.

He thought again of the broken voice in the night.

Come back. Come back to me.

That had been her voice, calling to him. Astonishment came over him. Realizing the truth had been a matter of logical deduction, but he hadn't counted on the depth of emotion that had driven her to confront the dragon. She carried so much passion, so much light.

For him.

I miss my mate with all my heart, and I would do anything or give anything to get him back again.

She had been talking about him. No one had ever

given him such devotion before—no one that he could remember. Over centuries uncounted, they had given him fear and hatred, and sometimes obeisance, and he had considered all of that his due.

And she had brought him diamonds, sapphires and gold. He stared at the sapphire color of her eyes and the gold of her hair. His favorite things.

He didn't know he was capable of compassion, until that moment. He said, as gently as he could, "No, I still haven't remembered."

Her gaze widened and drifted away, as if not knowing where to land, because wherever she looked, all she saw was the same horror.

That look drove through him like a spike.

He stepped over the fire, commanding it not to burn, and obedient to his will, the flames drew aside. Crouching in front of her, he put a hand underneath her chin, forcing her to look at him. He asked, "Why didn't you say something before now?"

She put a hand lightly against his forearm, stroking him, and even amidst his heat and anger, the action soothed him.

"How on earth could I tell you something like that, and hope you would possibly believe me?" she asked. "I mean, think a minute—you had a difficult time accepting the fact that I brought the gifts in good faith. How do you think it would have gone down if a total stranger had walked up to you and said, 'Oh hi, sorry about your head injury, by the way, I'm your mate'?"

He had pinned her underneath one claw. He had

been fully prepared to kill her as she drew close to him. He demanded, "When did it happen?"

"Last year. We've been together fourteen months."

"And the building that's under construction?"

She moistened her lips. "It's a—that's another complicated concept."

He growled under his breath. "That response is not acceptable any longer."

"Sometimes that response is all I can give you," she told him. "Your loss of memory is not just about me, Dragos. There is a lot you can't recall, and I can't just tell you in a sentence or two about things that are based on years of emotions, commitments, and understandings." She gripped his wrist. "You've lost memories of an entire life, involving a lot of people. Do you remember what I said about enemies earlier? Not only is that true, but it's also true about friends. You have friends. You have people who care about you."

He stared at her.

Widening her eyes, she lifted her shoulders in a shrug. "I know, go figure. It's hard to believe, isn't it?"

"We've built a life for ourselves," he said slowly, experimenting with the words.

"We *are* building a life for ourselves," she whispered. "And we're not going to give up on it, just because we've had a bad couple of days. Or when one of us loses his memories for a while and gets a little bitey."

His eyes narrowed. "What are you talking about?"

"Never mind," she muttered.

The whole conversation was bizarre, and part of him

wanted to reject it out of hand. He was a loner by nature, and suspicious for many centuries-old reasons.

It crossed his mind again that she could still be manipulating him, somehow, for her own gain. Setting aside the question of why she would do so, he thought of how she could have done it.

Perhaps she had found a way to cloak all of her lies in some sort of truthspell. Perhaps she was trying to lure him into some kind of trap. Perhaps *she* was the trap.

His gaze traveled again to the braid of hair at his wrist, and the gold ring on his finger. As much as he loved owning jewelry, he had never worn any, until apparently now. And that ring was a wedding ring.

For any kind of subterfuge to be employed at this sophisticated level, she would have needed to slip both wedding ring and braid onto his human form before he had been injured, and somehow gotten him to put a protection spell on the braid.

Really, that entire scenario strained his credulity.

But on the other hand, so did the thought of having a mate.

A wife.

A life full of complicated concepts, involving friendships.

Letting all of those thoughts go, he concentrated on the reality at hand.

The reality was, he held her life literally in one hand, his long fingers resting against the warm, soft skin underneath her chin. Her pulse beat delicately against his hand, and there was no fear anywhere in her eyes, or in her scent. She leaned forward into his touch, as if she wanted his hands on her skin.

She had no weapons or barriers of any kind. She had no magic spells, just her own wild, inherent Power that brushed with such a tantalizing coolness against the heat of his own.

"So we were building a life together," he said in a husky voice into her upturned face, as he stroked his fingers along her petal-soft skin. "Fine. I want to see it for myself."

With a growing predatory hunger, he watched her lovely mouth shape her words. "What do you mean?"

"I presume we have a home somewhere. Take me there. Show it to me." Lifting one shoulder, he added a touch of persuasion to his voice. "Maybe if I see it in person, it could jog my memory."

The painful, excruciatingly bright hope came back to life in her eyes, along with a multitude of other, more complex emotions that he couldn't decipher.

Complex emotions, no doubt, that went along with their complex life.

He didn't care about any of it. He only cared about one thing.

The other Dragos—the one with his memories intact—had somehow won this remarkable creature's heart and soul. Perhaps it was more than a touch insane to be jealous of himself, but he was.

He wanted what that other Dragos had. *She* was the real treasure, more precious than sapphires, diamonds and gold.

At the core of his ancient, cynical heart, he was an acquisitive creature, after all.

Chapter Six

"I THINK GOING home is a great idea," Pia said slowly.

For such an unbearable nightmare, things were actually beginning to look up. Dragos had shapeshifted into his human form, and he was talking to her. Really talking, not growling or roaring (or biting), or barking orders.

Also, she was intensely relieved that he had figured out the nature of their relationship for himself. He didn't feel any of the emotions, and that hurt like a burning knife had been thrust into her chest, but at least she didn't have to try to find some way to tell him and watch any possible disbelief cross his expression.

Her lips were dry. She hadn't hydrated enough after her climb, and she moistened them with the tip of her tongue. His gaze dropped to the small movement and grew intent, although his hard expression remained closed to her scrutiny.

He was still so suspicious, and that hurt too. Her own logic scolded her. Of course he would be suspicious. Suspicion was part of the dragon's nature. He had been a solitary creature for so long, with a predatory nature and an ancient, primitive past, and he was quick to war. He had a history of enemies that went back millennia.

This present mess wasn't his fault. None of this was anybody's damned fault. It was just a random, horrible accident that had happened, but it was still hard for her not to take things personally.

She had to stay braced. Seeing their house might not help his memories to return, but it might just help him to relax and learn to trust her a bit more. Anything would be better than the cold, confrontational attitude with which he had greeted her earlier.

He still touched her, the hard fingers of his hand curled under her chin. She still touched him, her own hand curled around his muscled forearm.

He would never let an enemy remain in such intimate contact with him. The realization fed the stubborn hope of hers that refused to die.

She gave him a tentative smile. "When would you like to leave?"

He didn't return the smile. That fierce gold gaze of his never left her mouth. "Now."

Nodding, she stood and glanced down at the fire. "I guess we didn't need to build this after all."

He straightened when she did, with that quick, lithe grace of his that belied his muscular bulk. "That remains to be seen," he said shortly. He passed a hand over the fire, and his Power flexed, dampening the flames. "It will still be here if needed."

Clenching her muscles, she forced herself not to

flinch. Of course, just because he wanted to see their home didn't mean he was committed to staying there.

At least, not yet.

Walking to her pack, she dug in the side pocket for the satellite phone. As Dragos watched, she punched in Graydon's number. When Graydon answered, she told him, "We're going back to the house now."

Graydon said carefully, "That sounds promising."

She could tell by the neutrality in his voice and words that Graydon knew very well Dragos could hear everything he said. Pia glanced at Dragos, who watched her every move with a sharp frown.

She told Graydon, "It's great news. I didn't want you to worry. I'll call when I can."

"Make it soon, okay?"

Dragos prowled close. He growled, "Who was that male?"

Was that a touch of jealousy? She didn't dare smile, but for the first time in almost two days, the heaviness in her heart lightened a little.

She also wasn't sure what to make of the fact that he didn't remember Graydon. She and Dragos had only been together fourteen months, but he had known Graydon for much, much longer. The damage to his memory seemed profound.

Meeting his fierce gaze, she told him calmly, "That was one of your best friends. He's been worried about both of us."

"I want to know his name." He gripped her upper arm.

She glanced down at his hand. The gesture was possessive, aggressive, yet his touch was gentle on her bare skin. Thank God, he had lost the impulse to violence.

She covered his hand with hers. "His name is Graydon, and he loves you very much."

"I want to meet him." His jaw tightened, and so did his fingers. "But not tonight. Where do we go?"

"Do you remember how to get back to the scene where you got hurt?" She studied him, uncertain how he would take the information. "It's about fifteen miles from here. You were pretty disoriented when you left yesterday."

His expression closed down. "Yes."

She hated when he shut her out like that. She couldn't tell what he was thinking. Tightening her lips, she said, "The accident happened roughly two hundred yards away from our house, on the other side of some bordering trees."

He remained silent for so long, she started to worry. He had thought he'd been attacked there. What if he refused to go anywhere near the construction site?

Finally, he replied, "I'll take us there."

Before she could do much other than nod her consent, he shapeshifted into the dragon again, his Wyr form filling up the clearing. He didn't give her time to gather up her pack. Instead, he scooped her into one of his forepaws, crouched and launched.

Clutching at one of his talons, she narrowed her eyes against the warm summer wind. Telepathically, she said, *You left your gold and jewels behind.*

Along with her satellite phone, in her pack. While she didn't want to mention that fact, she fretted at losing the ability to call Graydon. Just knowing she had the sat phone with her had felt like a lifeline.

High overhead, Dragos's head arched on his long, strong neck as he glanced behind them. His reply was telepathic as well. *That mountainside is deserted. I'll return soon enough for it, before anyone else has a chance to find it.*

Discouragement crushed down on her. Bracing one elbow on the curve of his claw, she rested her forehead in her hand. He wasn't just leaving the door open for a way out. He was actively planning on leaving again.

When he left again, would he let her come?

At that, the focus of her questions shifted drastically.

Would he allow her to leave him? What about Liam?

Her anxious thoughts ground to a halt. She didn't have any answers, only questions.

They fell silent. The dragon's powerful wingspread made short work of the distance back.

As they had talked, the moon had risen and silvery moonlight illuminated the countryside. A scattering of lights crisscrossed the land, following roads and highlighting houses. The scenery reminded her of the artwork that hung in his offices in New York.

When they neared their land, he slowed and circled, approaching the area in an oblique fashion. She had no doubt he was searching the area with all of his considerable senses, but she already knew what he would find.

Nothing, and no one. The property had been abandoned the day before, and except for a few safety lights, their house lay dark and deserted. Patiently, she waited for him to arrive at the same conclusion.

Apparently he did, for in an abrupt change of course, he landed in the wide clearing in front of the house and set her on her feet. As she watched, he changed back into his human form and strode over to take her arm again.

"A lot of people were here recently," he said. "Where did they go?"

"We knew you weren't thinking clearly." *Snapped at her.* She closed her eyes, willing the nightmarish image away. "But we also knew the dragon might come back. I ordered everyone to stay away until I told them they could return."

She took him up to the house. As they approached, his glittering gaze took in everything—the darkened, empty trailers a short distance away, the few cars that were still parked to one side of the house, the piles of building materials, two Caterpillar tractors resting at the edge of the nearby tree line.

Pausing on the front step, he turned to look over the clearing again, and he made a low sound of frustration at the back of his throat.

"Why do I remember some things and not others?" he muttered. "Those are cars. Those two vehicles are bulldozers. This apparatus attached to the side of the house is scaffolding. You called your friend on a satellite phone. You lit the fire with a BIC lighter. All those details are readily available, yet I wouldn't know my own name if you hadn't told me."

Heart aching, she shook her head. "I don't know. The mind is a complicated, mysterious thing. We could consult with doctors who specialize in traumatic brain injuries. They might be able to help."

Other than giving her one quick, frowning glance, he didn't respond to her suggestion. Instead, he grasped the doorknob and turned it. The door was unlocked. He pushed it open.

Twisting her hands together, she followed him into the house. Inside, the renovating materials—ladders, drop cloths, cans of paint and various tools—had been stacked neatly to the sides of the open spaces.

Silently, Dragos strode through the ground floor. She followed, flicking on light switches as they went.

His pace picked up until she had to trot to keep up with him. He paused in the doorway of his large, state-of-the-art office, and she hovered at his shoulder. "My scent is all over this room."

She told him, "That's because this room is yours, and you spend a lot of time in here. It's one of those complicated concepts."

His jaw flexed. She thought of all the places he would want to explore, that room would be at the top of the list, but after one more sweeping glance, he left it and moved on, prowling through the rest of the house, his presence brooding and intense.

She followed him everywhere he wanted to go—out on the patio, through the palatial kitchen, downstairs to the lower level.

Once, he paused for long moments in the hallway

just outside of the hidden panic room. Hope surged again as she watched him. It was an exhausting, out-of-control feeling, as if it was a creature that existed entirely separate from her own needs or wishes.

But he said nothing, and after a few moments, he moved on.

Nerves started to get to her when he took the stairway up to the second floor. She felt strung out, as if she had drunk too much caffeine for too many days. At the top of the stairs he hesitated and turned right. Her heart started to pound, and her hands shook.

She thought, I should say something. I need to warn him.

"You're afraid." He said it over one wide shoulder as he strode down the hall, past empty bedrooms with open doors.

"Not afraid, exactly," she replied tensely.

"Then what—exactly?"

With impeccable instincts, he paused at the closed door of Liam's nursery and assessed her expression.

She rubbed the corner of her mouth with unsteady fingers. "It's another one of those complicated concepts."

He opened the door and walked inside. And froze.

Wrapping her arms around her torso, she gripped her elbows tightly as she watched him from the doorway. The line of his back, from his wide shoulders arrowing down to narrow hips, was taut.

After one pulsing second, he tore through the rest of the rooms. She rushed after him.

He stopped in Peanut's bedroom, staring at the bright colors on the walls, the crib, the dresser with the changing pad and diapers. Liam's favorite stuffed animal, his bunny, lay in the crib. Evidently, Hugh and Eva had forgotten to grab it when everyone evacuated.

Dragos picked it up and briefly buried his face in it. His hands clenched on the soft toy until the broad knuckles turned white.

The silence had turned deafening. She hurt everywhere. Her body physically hurt. She didn't know where to look, or how to hold herself in such a way that the pain would lessen.

He whispered, "This is a male scent. I have a son."

The words struck the room as loud as a shout. She swallowed hard, and her voice shook as she said, "Yes."

He looked in the direction of the changing table. "He's small."

Again, she said, "Yes."

He turned to her, his gaze incandescent and raw. "How is that possible? How could I not remember I have a son?"

"I don't know." She hadn't intended to say anything, but her words acquired a life of their own and wrenched themselves out of her. "I don't know how you could forget either of us. *You're in my bones.*"

He jerked toward her, Liam's bunny still gripped in one fist. "Where is he?"

She put her head in her hands. "He's in the city."

"Because of me," he said through clenched teeth. He cut through the air with one hand. "Because I might have come back here to attack you. He was in danger because of me."

His violent emotions beat against her skin, an invisible force, until she felt bruised all over. She needed to lean on something.

There was nowhere to go that would be strong enough to brace her against the volcanic force raging in front of her—nowhere but forward. Blindly, she walked until she collided into his chest. "Please stop," she whispered. "You aren't the bad guy. There isn't a bad guy in this situation. It's just a bad situation."

His arms came around her. That was what she needed, more than air, more than water. She leaned on his strength, and he held her tightly.

Something came down on the top of her head—his cheek. It touched her briefly then lifted away. His arms loosened.

"I need to see the construction site," he growled.

Stiffening her spine, she lifted her head as she stepped back. The savagery in his expression took her aback until she realized what he really needed. He felt the need to fight, but there wasn't any enemy at hand, so he had focused on the only other thing available.

"All right," she told him. "Let's go. Let's do it now."

Pausing, he set the bunny on the dresser. His fingers seemed to linger on the toy's soft fur. Then he turned back to her, and they walked out of the nursery together.

There was only one other place in that wing that he hadn't explored, the closed door at the end of the hall. Glancing toward it, he looked an inquiry at her. She said briefly, "Those are our rooms."

He hesitated. Conflicting emotions evident in his reluctant pace, he walked to the door and opened it.

A little while ago, she had been braced for him walking into their suite. Now after the raw scene in Liam's nursery, she could hardly stand it. It felt worse than stripping her clothes off in front of a stranger, more revealing, and she couldn't breathe as she waited to hear what he would say.

What if he disliked it? What if he rejected it?

He didn't step over the threshold, but instead flipped on the light switch and stared for a long time at the room inside. His hands had clenched into fists again. He muttered, "This is *his* space with you."

She couldn't have heard him correctly. Shaking her head, she asked, "Excuse me, what did you say?"

Turning off the light again, he closed the door. "Never mind," he said. His expression had shut down again. Shutting her out again.

Suddenly wild to get out of that hall, with all of its happy memories, she walked rapidly back to the staircase and took the stairs two at a time. This time he was the one who followed her. She walked out the front of the house, never bothering to shut the front door, and strode down the path to the construction site by the lake.

To the place where her life had vanished.

He stayed close on her heels. She could sense him, a great inferno of heat prowling at her back. Within a few moments, they traversed the wooded area and walked out into clear air, at the edge of the site.

As she paused, Dragos came up by her side and they looked over the scene.

Nearby, the lake sparkled peacefully in the moonlight. This construction area was not neat, like the space around their house had been. Tools, hard hats and equipment had been abandoned, and across the clearing, the pile of rubble still lay strewn at the foot of the bluff.

She covered her mouth as she stared at the place, remembering the dread and panic.

Dragos took her by the hand, lacing his fingers with hers, and drew her forward until they stood together at the base of the bluff.

She fell into the past.

Digging bare-handed through the rubble. Hoping against hope.

She was so lost in the memory of her own nightmare, it took her a few moments to realize that the large, strong hand she gripped was trembling.

Pulled out of herself, she turned to face Dragos.

The frame of his body shook. In the moonlight, he looked drawn and ill.

"What is it?" Concerned, she rubbed his arm.

His bleak gaze met hers. He said hoarsely, "I snapped at you."

Of all the things she needed him to remember, that was the one thing she had hoped he never would.

She had a split second in which to decide how to respond. In that moment, she made a private vow to never talk about the experience.

How she had felt—the shock, the despair—was none of his business. At least she could protect him from that. They would each need to cope with their own issues that had arisen from what had happened, but for now, there was nothing else to do but confront this head-on.

Keeping her voice calm and reasonable, she said, "Well, of course you did. How else would you act? You had just suffered a massive blow to the head, and you thought you were under attack."

In the short amount of time they'd had together, they had shared some tough moments, but through it all, she had never seen him look so injured. He looked like he wanted to vomit.

"I almost killed you," he said from the back of his throat. "I could have killed you. What kind of Wyr could do that to his mate?"

He was breathing raggedly, as if he had been running for a long time.

"You didn't." She put her arms around his shaking body and held him in her strongest, tightest grip, turning her head so that her cheek rested in the slight hollow of his breastbone. "*You* wouldn't."

He made an inarticulate noise that sounded crushed, and clenched her to him.

"I still don't remember you," he whispered.

A few hours ago, hearing those words had wounded her terribly, but now she knew better.

She rubbed his back soothingly. "Yes, you do. Somewhere deep inside of you, you do. We just have to be patient and give this some time." Tilting back her head, she gave him a gentle smile. "Because I'm in your bones, too."

Chapter Seven

D RAGOS DIDN'T KNOW about that.

If she was in his bones, why did holding the delicate, feminine form in his arms feel entirely new? The perfumed scent of her hair was amazing. The trust she exhibited as she leaned against his body was revolutionary, life-changing.

He hadn't earned her trust. It was a gift, like her healing, and the gold and jewels. Her generosity of spirit staggered him.

The different aspects of his personality raged against each other. He felt torn, pulled in too many directions. Part of him strained for the memories that weren't there. He was shocked at so much evidence of his presence in this place, and furious that he could not feel a part of any of it.

Then there was the jealousy, which made him feel more insane than ever.

He hated the other Dragos, the one who had been a full participant in this rich, complex life. The one whom Pia obviously adored. He wanted to roar a challenge at that other dragon and tear him to shreds, until he was the only one left alive, the true victor and inheritor of all this bounty.

But there was no other dragon. There was only himself. The threat he sensed lay inside of him.

He was the one who had snapped at her. He could have killed her, without knowing, and then at some future date, he might have realized what he had done. He might have remembered that she was his mate. A cold nausea swept over him again at the thought.

"I'm sorry," he whispered into her. "I can't tell you how sorry I am. I didn't know. I could never have done it if I'd known."

She rubbed his back with one slender hand. When she spoke her voice remained as gentle and pragmatic as ever. "I know how sorry you are, and I knew you would be. What happened here—I never wanted you to remember that. All I want is for you to remember us."

Of course, she wanted her husband back. It seemed the time to say something reassuring, but he couldn't reconcile the warring parts of himself enough to verbalize anything that didn't sound completely crazy.

Things like, you are not his. You are mine.

I'll kill anyone who tries to take you away from me.

Forget the time you had with him. Be with me, here and now, not some image of who you think I am supposed to be.

Growling in frustration, he gave up on words entirely, tilted up her head and covered her mouth with his. Her body softened readily, eagerly, against his, and her lips parted for his invasion.

This response should be his, but he couldn't trust it.

The things he felt were dark, tangled, and edged in violence. She thought she was kissing her husband. Instead she was kissing a savage creature. One who might kill anyone, or do anything to have her.

He wrenched his mouth away, and she made a soft sound of protest that went straight to his heart and groin alike. For a moment he thought she might tug on him to coax his head back down to her, and a greedy, ravenous part of him needed her to do it, to show him that she wanted him.

See me. Choose me.

Instead, she let him go and stepped away.

"Do you need more time here?" She sounded breathless.

"No," he snapped. He watched her recoil, and part of him wanted to rampage through the night in a rage.

Cautiously, she peered sideways at him as she suggested, "Would you like to go back to the house?"

Back to the house, with the silent, empty nursery for an absent child, and the beautiful, serene suite of rooms *the other Dragos* shared with her.

Clenching his fists, he pressed them against his thighs. This was too volatile, even for him. He had to get in control of himself. How could he expect her to continue trusting him, if he didn't trust himself?

"Go on back." His tone was too short, and he fought to soften it. "I need a few minutes alone."

She hesitated, her face tilted up to his like some rare flower that only emerged in moonlight, and while she tried to hide her anxiety, he could still sense it running through her slender form. "Are you sure?"

With a sudden flash of intuition, he realized what she was worried about. He touched her face. The softness of her skin was addicting. This time, when he reached for gentleness, it came to him readily. "I'm not going to leave," he murmured. "I only want a few minutes."

Her fingers curled around his, and she pressed her face into the palm of his hand. She said quietly, "Okay. I'll see you back at the house."

Some predatory instinct had him gripping the delicate angle of her chin, carefully to avoid bruising that soft skin. He said into her face, "I didn't want to stop kissing you."

The tiny sound of her indrawn breath brushed over his heated skin. Her heartbeat pulsed against the tips of his fingers. She whispered, "I didn't want to pull away."

I'm not who you think I am.

I am not the man you so badly want me to be.

He didn't say it. Instead, he brushed her soft mouth with his lips, and never mind that he really was *the other Dragos*—this impulse to sensual intimacy was all new. It was the first time it had ever existed in his world, and trapped in a tangle of his own devising, the dragon had no idea how to tell her that.

Letting go of his hand, she stepped back, pivoted on her heel and walked back to the house.

He stared at her retreating form, his muscles tightening instinctively as she disappeared underneath the shadow of the trees. Once he was truly alone, he gave in to the savage, jealous creature inside, shapeshifted back into the dragon and prowled over every inch of the construction site.

He didn't care what he looked at. He wasn't searching for any kind of evidence of wrongdoing. That suspicion had been thoroughly laid to rest. The dragon simply picked through the rock and various items for something to do while the real activity happened inside his massive, convoluted mind.

He hadn't left the gold and jewels back up the mountain for safekeeping. He had forgotten about it, and he'd only remembered when she had brought it up.

Which, he would have said, was rather unlike him. He never forgot about treasure. Never. Except for this time, when all of his attention had been focused on the real treasure in front of him.

There was only one creature he'd ever heard of who could heal with her blood, a creature that had long ago disappeared into myth and legend, and yet he knew that must be her true nature. He knew it like he knew how to make the fire respond to his commands.

Leaving the construction site, he leaped into a short flight that took him over the barrier of trees and landed in the clearing on the other side. Once grounded, he cloaked his presence in case she watched for him and prowled around the massive house.

Look at the scene, so civilized. So pretty.

The lights she had left on for him twinkled in the darkness.

His tail whipped back and forth as he bared his teeth at the house. He did not fit in that civilized, pretty life.

He fit out here in the night, where the moon created a world filled with shadows, and other predators knew to slink away at the first sign of his presence.

Dragos.

Cuelebre.

Those were his names, and they said what he was. No more, no less, yet everywhere in that house he had seen the evidence of a civilized man, the man she had mated with, the man who might never return to her.

The man he hated and would kill if he could. The man he did not want to be.

But he did want to take that man's place in those soft, serene rooms upstairs. That private place, filled with cream furniture and jewel-toned colors, and all the sensual evidence of her nesting. The perfume she wore. The scatter of feminine clothes, and shoes, and jewelry.

Most especially, he wanted to take that man's wife for his own.

So he would put up with the rest of the civilized life. He would figure out the complexities in that office of his and learn to make peace with the many other creatures who seemed to be part of the total package. Tilting his head, he shapeshifted back into his human form and strode toward the house.

A better man, perhaps *the other Dragos* she had fallen in love with, might warn her of what he had become.

But he wasn't a better man. He wasn't a good man at all.

And unfortunately for her, he was the one who wore her ring on his finger.

Entering by the front door, he tracked her to the back of the house, where he found her in the kitchen, sitting at the table and eating a bowl of cereal.

She had showered, and her damp, combed hair followed the curve of her shapely head. Her sturdy hiking clothes were gone, and she wore thin, soft-looking pajama pants along with a matching sleeveless top that was a deep, ruby red that highlighted the golden tan of her skin. She was barefoot also, he saw, her pink-painted toenails peeping from underneath the hem of her pants.

Glancing at him self-consciously, she said, "If you're hungry, there's plenty of food in the fridge."

He was on fire with hunger, but not for food. He watched her ravenously as she spooned the last bite of her cereal into her mouth. The way her plump, naked lips slipped around her spoon as she took the last bite of food gave him an incredibly painful erection.

Clenching, he fought for self-control. She had undergone a lot of stress, and to the best of his knowledge hadn't eaten anything for a long time. "How about you?" the dragon asked, striving for a solicitous tone. "Is there anything else you would like to eat?"

Her large gaze slid sideways to him, and he could tell by her guarded expression that he wasn't acting quite right. "No, thank you. I've had enough."

As she slid out of her seat and carried her bowl and spoon to the sink, his gaze dropped to her shapely ass and thighs, the tight glide of toned muscle sliding sinuously underneath the thin material of her pants.

Abruptly, he said, "I know what you are. I knew

when you healed me."

Setting her bowl in the sink, she turned to face him, her teeth worrying at her lower lip. "I wasn't really trying to hide it from you, although you should know—we hide it from everybody else."

He wasn't surprised. In her Wyr form, her horn could dispel any poison. She could heal with her blood. She could only be captured by unfair means. No cage could hold her. Her life sacrificed could bestow immortality. If word got out about what kind of creature she was, she would be hunted for the rest of her life.

He stalked across the room toward her, slowly so as not to frighten her. Cocking his head, he studied her closely. "You're cloaking yourself somehow. I didn't notice it before. I know how to cloak my presence, but I have never seen someone with the ability to cloak as subtly as you do."

While she might not have realized it consciously yet, some deep, animal part of her sensed that he had gone on the hunt, and she shifted her body restlessly as she leaned back against the kitchen counter. "My mom always said our cloaking was the most important thing we could do for ourselves. That, and knowing when to run and how to hide."

He would like to see her run. Not in fear, or because she felt she was in danger—those thoughts were as distasteful to him as the scent of her tears. But the thought of chasing her down a dark forest path as she tried her best to elude him... that was a game that appealed to every hunter's instinct he had, and his erection hardened.

Stepping in front of her, he trapped her against the sink by putting one hand on the counter on either side of her torso. This close, he could hear how her pulse picked up and her breathing shortened. Of all the many revelations in this long struggle of the day, the fact that he could smell her arousal for him was one of the most amazing.

The warmth from her body was a gentle heat that bathed the air against his skin. "Take the cloaking spell off," he said, in a voice that had turned low and husky. "I want to see you for who you really are."

A small smile tugged at the corner of her lips. "You never have tolerated any barriers between us."

He frowned, not sure how much he liked the comparison between himself and *the other Dragos*, but before he could decide how to respond, that elegant, subtle cloaking spell of hers fell away.

Pale, delicate illumination shone from her skin. He lost every other impulse and stared. The glow was so much like the moon's silvery glow, yet it was exponentially more precious, as it was drenched with her cool, witchy magic.

He lost himself in awe. The dragon couldn't remember the last time he had ever felt awe. Perhaps he had felt it once at the morning of the world, in that first, bright dawn. Gently taking one of her hands, he lifted it to his mouth, marveling in the effortless symmetry of the movement in her graceful wrist and arm.

She adapted to his action and took it for her own, as

she raised her hand to cup the side of his face. That magic, the immediacy of her presence, sank into his skin and found its way into his old, wicked soul. Forgetting to breathe, he closed his eyes and soaked her in greedily.

"What do you need now, Dragos?" she asked softly. "Do you know? Do you need space, or your own place to sleep? Or do you want to go back to the mountaintop?"

The swiftness of his internal reaction jolted him, an immediate whiplash of denial at the thought of taking his own space, but when she mentioned going back to the mountaintop, he had to pause.

He couldn't deny it. He was tempted. The stone of the ledge would still be radiating heat from the day's sun, and the gigantic canopy of the night sky would arc overhead, stars gleaming like diamonds. The wildness and solitude of the place called him, and he knew she would come with him if he asked.

Yet, while he wanted to return at some point to collect the small pile of treasure—his gifts—going back there now would not be conquering the alien landscape of this place, and that was what he was most determined to do. He needed to invade that private place upstairs, the nest she had shared with *the other Dragos*, and to claim it for his own.

He needed to claim her in that space.

Holding her gaze, he said deliberately, "I need to take you to bed."

The sense of her arousal deepened, and the light that came into her face in that moment had nothing to do with her own magic, and everything to do with the magic they were creating between them. She whispered, "I'm glad."

Keeping hold of her hand, he turned and they walked through the silent house together.

Chapter Eight

P IA DIDN'T KNOW what to think of Dragos's deliberate, sensual approach, or the way they journeyed upstairs hand in hand.

It should have felt like a sedate pace. It didn't. It felt like a slow burn that crawled underneath her skin and set her on fire.

As they passed Peanut's nursery, he glanced at the closed door, and the expression in his eyes turned moody. "I need to see him too," he said. "But not yet. First, I need to be more settled in myself."

After a pause to think it over, she replied, "That's an excellent idea. The accident was only yesterday afternoon—it's been barely over a day. Much as I miss him, he's surrounded by people who love him, and I know they're doing a wonderful job looking after him. It's okay to take a few days, maybe even a week." She looked up at him. "The most important thing right now is to make sure you get what you need."

He opened the door to their suite, set a flattened hand at the small of her back and ushered her inside. Biting a nail, she watched him explore the rooms, discovering for himself where everything was. Silently, he disappeared into his walk-in closet for a few moments, then he strode into the bathroom. A moment later, she heard the sound of water running.

If the situation had been normal, he would never have let go of her hand. She would have gone with him and offered him comfort and sex. They would have shared healing intimacy in that shower. They had certainly done so several times before.

Now everything was so strange. He advanced on her and made no secret of his sensual interest, and yet he had barriers that remained in some deep, fundamental way. It confused her and made her question her own instincts.

He acted like Dragos, but he didn't act like *her* Dragos.

Eyes filling with tears, she went to the balcony doors, opened them wide and stepped outside for some fresh air. He didn't know about the healing, intimate times they had shared in the shower together, and she didn't feel confident enough to go into the bathroom to join him, even though she wanted to. She didn't know how to act, and she was afraid of doing something wrong, something that might send him away.

She didn't hear him step out onto the balcony. Not only was he fast and light on his feet, but he was also extraordinarily quiet when he chose to be.

Something else alerted her, a huge, fierce Power brushing against her senses.

Wiping her face, she kept her gaze fixed firmly on the shadowed mountain range in the distance.

"You could leave, you know," she said. "Be free,

start a completely new life. You have an out like nobody has ever had in the history of Wyr mating."

Also, just because they had mated, that didn't mean they had to live together. Several different species of Wyr chose not to live with their mates. Solitary by nature, they kept their lives separate and came together only when they needed.

She didn't want to live that way. She couldn't imagine adapting to that after the wealth of what they had shared, but you never knew what you could live with once you didn't have any choice. If that was what it took to keep him in her life, she would do it.

His hands clamped down on her shoulders, and he spun her around.

He was naked, his inky black hair and dark bronze skin still damp. His clean, male scent wafted over her. She got only a blurred impression of his muscled body before he jerked her toward him, bending over her upturned face.

His expression had turned murderous, and the gold in his eyes glowed bright and hot.

"Fuck that," he hissed.

Aw, he said the sweetest things to her.

Patting his hair-sprinkled chest, she said unsteadily, "I didn't say you *should*, or even that I wanted you to. I said you *could*. I only meant to point out this situation is really bizarre."

He thrust that deadly face into hers, growling, "I keep what is mine. I don't leave it. I don't lose it, not ever, and I go after anyone who tries to take it from me."

She knew that quite well, which was one of the major reasons she had chosen not to tell him that she had once stolen from him. That, in fact, him chasing after her had been how they had first met.

Being that it was another one of those complicated concepts and all, and best appreciated in context.

She should say something to lighten the mood. She should reach for the gentle, pragmatic way with which she had responded to his traumatized reaction at the site of the accident.

But her pragmatic side was worn out. It had gotten its ass kicked over the last two days. All of a sudden, she didn't have any more coping ability left, and even though she tried to stop the tears from coming, her damn eyes sprang a leak.

Her voice wobbled, and her mouth shook. "That's just it—you don't have any of those memories anymore that make me yours."

If anything, he looked even more furious. "What happened to 'I'm in your bones'?"

"Well, I want it to be true, but I don't know that it is, do I? And I'm t-tired."

"Stop that," he demanded. "Stop."

He cupped her face. Despite the roughness of his tone, his hands were infinitely gentle as he wiped the paths of her tears with both thumbs.

Belatedly she realized he was ordering her to stop crying, and a hiccup of laughter broke out of her. It quickly twisted into something else.

"I thought you were dead," she sobbed. "I stood in

front of that horrible pile of rock and thought you were dead, and all I wanted to do was crawl under that pile to join you."

His hard features turned stricken. The world tilted as he scooped her into his arms and carried her into the bedroom.

He laid her on the bed and came down over her, pinning her with his heavy body. She craved his weight. Gripping the back of his head, she dug her fingers through his silky black hair, holding on to him tightly.

His mouth came down on hers, stopping her uncontrolled flood of words.

Hardened lips slanted over hers, and his tongue plunged into her mouth. There was no finesse, no coaxing. This was a taking, and she reached for it with all of her greedy heart, kissing him back with everything she had inside of her. All the love, all the desire.

Bunching his fists in the bedspread on either side of her head, he thrust a heavy, muscled thigh between hers. The hard weight of his erection lay against her pelvis, and she reached for it, caressing the broad, velvet head with one shaking hand.

He hissed into her mouth, and his hips pushed against hers rhythmically.

She pushed back, matching his rhythm. Pulling his mouth from hers, he rose onto his knees and shredded the clothes from her body.

When she was completely naked, he froze. The quality of his stillness made her pause, and she searched his expression.

He was staring at her.

Their bedroom lay in shadows. The only illumination came from the moonlight shining in through the windows, and from her.

The pearly luminescence shone from every inch of her. It had been a part of her since birth. It served no purpose. Like the color of her hair, or her eyes, it simply was. Often she had been exasperated with it, and sometimes fearful for what it gave away about her nature.

It was the most dangerous fact of her existence, the most likely thing to betray her. She could never let down her guard or relax her cloaking spell, unless she was absolutely sure she was in a private, safe place.

All of that melted away in the face of the wonder in Dragos's expression. With one hand, he touched the swelling curve of her breast, circling the pink jut of her nipple with the tips of his callused fingers.

With the other hand, he stroked the curve of her slender waist and the swell of her hip. The golden curls at the juncture of her thighs grew damp with the full, sharp ache of desire.

She never realized how empty she was until she was with him. Then the emptiness pierced her, and he was the only one who could ease the ache.

"You're the most gorgeous thing I have ever seen." His words were barely audible.

Grasping his large, hard penis in one glowing hand, she stroked his length and whispered, "You're the most gorgeous thing I've ever seen too."

His powerful frame was bound with heavy muscles.

He was a dark, shadowy figure in the moonlit room, the bulk of his body defined by even darker shadows—the silken black hair sprinkled across his broad chest and arrowing down to his groin, the ripple of his abdominals and biceps as he crawled over her, the long indentation of flesh at his hips.

He didn't stop until he caged her with his body, pausing on his hands and knees over her. It was a dominant, possessive posture, and she loved it. Running her hands hungrily over him, she touched his flat, male nipples and petted the sprinkle of hair on his chest, following the path it made down to his groin.

His heavy, thick erection hung down to her, and underneath it, his sac had drawn tight. She circled the base of his penis and stroked his testicles, intending to slide down the bed between his legs and take him in her mouth, but he had other plans.

Taking her by the chin, he tilted her face up to his, making her look at him as he parted her legs and settled between them. His gaze burned with incandescence.

He said softly, "You are mine. You are always going to be mine. It doesn't matter what came before, the only thing that matters is what is now and going forward. There will never be anyone else for you. Only me. *Me*."

A part of her marveled at the strange emphasis he put on those words, but it was overwhelmed by the huge tide of other feelings. Gladness, fierce joy and gratitude were foremost among them.

"Of course I am. I always have been, I always will be."

Until death might call an end to their lives, but even then, death couldn't part them. They were Wyr, mated for life.

One or the other of them might linger to finish their affairs. When she thought Dragos might be gone, she had made that commitment, silently, to Liam. She cherished the fact that her mother had done that for her before leaving this earth, and she would do no less for her son.

But in the end, she would always orbit around Dragos, always look for him, always reach for him. Whatever bridge he crossed, whatever journey he might make, she would always follow.

His rough-hewn features and body clenched tight, as he focused on some internal landscape only he could see. Sprawling over her, he burrowed his face into her neck and sought her skin with his mouth, while he reached between her legs to finger the plump, delicate folds of her sex.

He sucked, licked, bit at her, his sharp teeth causing a light, erotic sting. "This is mine," he muttered into the curve of her breast before he suckled her nipple. "This, and this."

Gripping his shoulders, she jerked and shuddered under the sensual onslaught.

"Yes," she told him.

Yes, and yes.

Breathing heavily, he rested his forehead against her breastbone. "What lies inside this body is mine."

He was claiming all of her.

She lifted her head off the bed. "Dragos," she said, even as he probed and stroked her slick, private flesh.

He paused and tilted his head to look up at her. His brilliant gaze was jealous, secretive. For the love of all the gods, what on earth was going on in that convoluted mind of his?

She so adored this difficult, arrogant man.

In a strong, sure voice, she told him, "You are mine, too. You always will be. I'll never give up or let go, no matter how many times you get bonked on the head, or how exasperating you become."

She could say some pretty sweet things too, when she put her mind to it.

Satisfaction flashed across his face, along with triumph, and his reaction caught her attention, confusing her all over again. After all, it wasn't as though she had made any secret of how she felt about him.

She didn't have time to puzzle over it for long. Holding her gaze deliberately, he penetrated her with two fingers. She was so ready for him he didn't need to draw out any moisture.

The sensation of his fingers gliding into her felt so good, so necessary, she braced her heels against the mattress and lifted her hips up to his touch.

It caused him to growl underneath his breath. He fucked her with his fingers, intently watching every nuance of her expression. When the ball of his thumb came in contact with her clitoris, she shattered into a million pieces.

Her eyes dampened. When she could talk again, she

murmured, "I guess there were some other things you didn't forget."

"It must be like riding a bicycle." He hesitated with a frown. "Except I don't think I ride bicycles."

At that, she burst out laughing and wrapped her arms around him. "No, darling, you don't ride bicycles."

He lunged at her, a quick, predatory swoop, and captured her mouth. Kissing her so deeply, he pushed her into the mattress, while at the same time he gripped his penis and rubbed the thick, broad head against her fluted opening. She lost her laughter in anticipation.

He pushed into her, and it was everything she knew and needed for it to be. Familiarity and recognition only made it sweeter and stronger, and she had room enough to ache for him that he had lost that deep, strong experience.

Then that thought fled, as he filled her to the brim, not stopping until he had sunk all the way into her, to the root. His hips flexing at the bowl of her pelvis, he clenched his teeth and muttered, "I can't get deep enough."

She knew that pained intensity. She had felt it so many times herself.

There was only one way she knew to make it better. Putting her mouth to his ear, she whispered, "Try."

Growling, he started to move. With an instinct that went deeper than thought, she picked up his rhythm and matched it, lifting her hips for his thrusts.

Hauling her up briefly, he angled one arm underneath her torso, his forearm sliding up between her shoulder blades as he sank his fist into her hair. With his other hand, he gripped her by the hip as he fucked her harder.

So possessive. She embraced all of it, the slight awkwardness of the position, the tight grasp he had on her body.

The tension was building again. Raking her fingernails down his back, she egged him on. "Harder."

He responded immediately, pistoning in deliberate thrusts. Their bodies dampened with sweat. This wasn't sweet, slow lovemaking. It was fierce and desperate.

Greedy, she was so greedy. She was frustrated she didn't get a chance to climax again. He plunged ahead of her to the finish, arcing up with a gasp as he spurted into her.

Letting go of her own need, she embraced him and focused on his pleasure. She felt every gorgeous pulse of his penis. Trying to make it last for him, she gripped him as tightly as she could with her inner muscles.

He came to a halt, breathing raggedly. She stroked the back of his neck.

His fingers loosened in her hair, and he came up onto his elbows. He looked agonized, desperate.

He said roughly, "I'm not done."

She stared. Before she could respond, he hauled her up bodily and flipped her so that she came onto her hands and knees. Incredulously, she complied, arching her back and tilting her ass in primal invitation.

Always when he penetrated her from behind, he felt bigger, and he seemed to get deeper. He entered her with a growl that vibrated down her spine. A nearly inaudible whine came out of her in response.

Oh God, oh God. This was a miracle she didn't even know to hope for.

Pleasure and emotion rocketed through her body. It was her turn to clench fistfuls of the bedspread. His hands clamped down on to her hips, and as he fucked her, she buried her face in the material to muffle the sound of her sob.

He was mating.

Maybe he didn't remember their life together, but he was mating with her.

That was the last true coherent thought she had before the swell of her own mating frenzy took her over. Her climax came over her like a steamroller. She flung back her head, gasping at the intensity of it.

Just when she thought the peak had passed, he wrapped an arm around her and found her clitoris with his fingers, and she exploded again. Clawing at his thigh, she urged him on.

This time his thrusts sent her against the headboard. She tried to brace herself, but she wasn't in control. Neither of them were. As he came again too, an animal sound wrenched out of him.

Silence stole into the room, and stillness. It was a chance to catch her breath.

But only for a moment.

He came down over her, spooning her so that his chest pressed against her back. She could feel his heart pounding against her skin, a powerful, rapid force.

Meanwhile, he remained planted deep inside of her, his erection as hard as ever.

She knew this dance. They had been through it before.

Dragos buried his face in her hair, as he whispered, "I'm still not done."

Chapter Nine

H E DREAMED OF being buried, lost in darkness. Beyond his grave, a splendid, graceful creature of shining, ivory light waited for him. She had delicate hooves and legs, and the single, slender horn on her forehead pierced him sweetly through the heart.

Come back, she called. *Come back to me.*

Yearning toward her, he struggled to free himself. Dust filled his nostrils, choking him. From an immeasurable distance across the starry night, Death, whose name was Azrael, turned to face him.

Azrael whispered his name.

Dragos was well acquainted with that old bastard. They were, after all, brothers. Azrael, also known as the Hunter, was a part of the dragon's nature, as Dragos was a part of his.

He said to Azrael, *You will not have me.*

Azrael gave him a pale, elegant smile. At times Death could appear quite alluring. Green eyes glittering, he said, *One day I might, brother. You are immortal, not Deathless, and nothing in this universe lasts forever.*

Opening his jaws wide, the dragon let out a furious roar, and Death vanished in a blast of heat and light.

DRAGOS WOKE WITH a start.

Sunlight poured through the large windows of the bedroom. Pia nestled against his side, her head resting on his arm. She was deeply asleep.

Shaking off the dream, he lifted his head and let his gaze roam down her nude body. Her luminescent glow was not quite as apparent in the bright light of day. Instead, her skin retained a faint, pearly sheen. While the effect was subtle, it was still all too obviously inhuman.

Her current position accentuated the hourglass shape of her body. She had marks on her skin, faint smudges of bruising and reddened scores of bite and scratch marks. She was already healing, and by midafternoon the marks would be gone completely.

A more civilized man would care that he had marked her. Perhaps *the other Dragos* would have cared. He touched one fading bruise lightly with his finger. Being neither of those two men, and intensely possessive, he would be sorry to see them disappear.

Then he regarded his own body. He was so much bigger than she, harder and more calloused, and yet he had marks on his skin too. As he shifted lazily against the sheets, the scratches she had made on his back reminded him of her own passionate response to him.

Carefully, so as not to wake her, he leaned over her sleeping form and mouthed, "You are so very much mine."

He was a fierce creature at the mildest of times. Now, the intensity of his feelings for her shook even him. And so, she was still a fool to have allowed it, let alone to have welcomed it as she had.

He eased her head off his arm and replaced it with a pillow. She never awakened. They had not stopped making love until well after dawn, and clearly he had worn her out.

Slipping out of bed, he went to the bathroom to sluice off quickly in the shower. After a few moments of searching in his closet, he located faded, cutoff jean shorts that he slipped on. He didn't bother with any other clothes, or with shoes. The summer day was already acquiring heat, and besides, they were alone on the estate.

He left her to search for food in the kitchen. The refrigerator was well stocked with both carnivore and vegan dishes that could be consumed with a minimum of effort. Someone had planned well for them.

Standing at the counter, he ate most of a roast chicken. Once the sharpest edge of his hunger had been satisfied, he went exploring.

The office—*the other Dragos's* office—drew him. He took his time discovering all the different components, glancing through file drawers, reading the first pages of contracts, studying building plans strewn all over a round, mahogany table. The construction site by the lake would be quite a compact complex when it was completed, combining both offices and living quarters.

Without having to be told, he knew that nothing left out in plain view would be vitally important. Any sensitive materials were either locked in the recessed wall safe he found hidden behind a paneling, or password protected on his computer, or hidden in the inaccessible recesses of his mind.

Raging against his lost memory was an exercise in futility. He clamped down on the emotion as he tried several combinations on the computer, yet failed to discover the right password.

What would *the other Dragos* use as a password? He would not fall into the trap of using personal or obvious information.

When another log-in attempt failed, his self-control slipped. Snarling, he swept everything off his desk and threw a stapler with such force it shot through a window.

The glass shattered and fell out of the window frame, just as Pia walked around one edge of the doorway, talking on a cell phone.

Stopping in midsentence, she came to an abrupt halt. Then she said into her phone, "I'll have to call you back later. I just wanted to let you know we'll need a few days here."

"I'll arrange everything," said the man on the other end of the call. "You concentrate on yourselves. Don't worry about a thing."

Graydon, the man's name was.

"Give Peanut all my love," Pia said.

All her love? Dragos's rage acquired a new focus. Who was this Peanut?

"I will," Graydon promised. "This is fantastic news, honey. I'll talk to you soon."

Her face calm and movements unhurried, she turned off her cell phone. She had showered too, Dragos saw, and had dressed in a cheerful outfit of yellow shorts and a light summer top splashed with big, bright sunflowers. Her hair was still damp, and she wore pretty flip-flop sandals with tiny yellow flowers etched into leather straps.

She looked like a happy creature of sunshine and light, while he was still seriously considering smashing the desktop computer to bits.

"You love someone called Peanut," he growled, his fists clenched. "Who the fuck has a name like Peanut?"

She flinched. Somehow, he had managed to strike a nerve. Tucking her phone into her pocket, she said quietly, "That's our son's nickname. I started calling him that when he was just a little bundle of cells. You know, because for a while he was just the size of a peanut. Anyway, it stuck. His real name is Liam."

He sucked in a breath. Pivoting away from her, he stared sightlessly out the window he'd broken.

She came up behind him and stroked his back. As soon as her fingers touched his bare skin, the last of his rage died. He bowed his head.

"What happened?" she asked gently.

He rubbed his face. "I can't figure out his password."

She paused, and when she spoke next, her voice had gentled even further. "*His* password?"

Tilting his head toward the sound of her voice, he realized what he had let slip.

His emotions surged again, a powerful cocktail of anger and frustration. All at once he let it go.

"Yes, *his* password," he snapped. He shrugged away

from her calming touch and rounded on her. "*The other Dragos.* The one who has a closet full of handmade suits upstairs. The one who reads contracts and negotiates treaties, and who debates the difference between Wolf and Viking appliances." He gestured violently at the appliance manuals that had been resting on the desk, and now lay scattered across the floor.

She bit her lip. It was not in laughter. She said softly, "You wanted to buy the best things for my kitchen."

The walls of the house closed in on him. Grabbing her hand, he snarled, "I've got to get out of here."

Moving rapidly, he dragged her out of the house. She didn't try to stop him. Instead, she trotted willingly at his side. As soon as they reached the open air, he let go of her hand, shapeshifted into the dragon, scooped her into one paw and launched.

Some flights are lazy, long spiraling glides through the air. This fight was a battle. His wings scything through the air, he flew as fast as he could back to the mountainside where he had rested the day before.

The ledge by the stream was just as they had left it, with the pile of his gifts, her pack underneath the trees, and the stack of firewood and partially burnt wood in the fire ring.

He landed, not gently, but caught himself up before he set her on her feet, which he did with deliberate care. Then he whirled away from her to pace.

She said nothing. Out of the corner of his eye, he watched her walk to her pack and settle in the shade of the tree, with her back braced against the trunk.

Tilting his head toward the sun, he considered leaving her and taking a solitary flight. But if he had truly wanted to be alone, the dragon would have left her back at the house, and she was clever enough to let him find his own way through his uncertain, surly mood.

At last, he gave in to the summer sun and stretched out his great length on the hot stone.

He said into the silence, "I am well aware of how crazy I sound."

He glanced at her sidelong. She had curled onto her side, knees tucked to her chest and head resting on her pack, watching him. Her expression was accepting, even compassionate. How could she look at him in such a way? She, of all people, should know that he was dangerous.

He demanded, "You do know that I am not that man, don't you?"

Finally, she spoke. "I believe that you are not the man you think you were."

Scowling, the dragon snapped, "What does that mean?"

"If you look at the details of his life without having his memories, I think it would be easy to get the wrong impression of who *that* Dragos is," she told him. Sitting up, she crossed her legs and toyed with a blade of grass. "The handmade suits, the contracts and negotiations... He didn't do all of that because he was civilized. He did it because he was playing the game." She met his gaze. "And you are very, very good at it."

Tapping his talons on the stone, he considered that.

Playing a game. Yes, he could understand that.

Rising up on his haunches, the dragon crawled over to her, bringing his head down until his snout came close to her face.

"I snapped at you," he whispered.

She cupped his snout and smiled up into his gaze. "I'm drawing a line right now. We have to agree to get over that. I know you're dangerous. I've always known you were dangerous. I was not naive about your nature when I mated with you the first time, and I am certainly not naive about it now. You never broke faith with me. *You* would never hurt me. What you did when you were injured and you couldn't recognize me is not anything we are going to worry about again."

A sense of peace threatened to take away his bad mood. He whuffled at her.

"I'm not ever going to be a good man," he warned.

She pressed a kiss to his snout. "We talked about that once, and I told you then—maybe you're not a good man, but you make a truly excellent dragon."

He muttered, "Maybe over time I can make peace with that other Dragos."

"If you give it a serious try, I think you'll be surprised at how well you do." She lifted a shoulder. "And if you can't adjust, maybe we'll go somewhere else and do other things. We're going to live a long time together, and things change."

The last of his tension eased away. Heaving an immense sigh, he shapeshifted and laid his head in her lap. She stroked her fingers through his hair, and for the first time since the accident, he fell into a truly deep, restful sleep.

✧   ✧   ✧

THE SUN TRAVELED across a blue, cloudless sky as Dragos slept.

After a while, she grew sleepy too, until finally she couldn't keep her eyes open any longer, and she nodded off, her hands laced protectively over the back of his head.

Sometime later, he began to stir, and she came awake with a jerk. She rubbed her eyes and looked around. They had dozed the afternoon away.

After nuzzling her thighs, he yawned and rolled onto his back. She gave him a smile as she flicked bits of grass off his skin.

He never got sunburned, no matter how long he stayed out in the sun. Instead, the dark bronze of his skin grew more burnished and rich. After a moment, all the bits of grass were gone and she gave up on that small excuse to touch him and simply stroked his bare chest.

He watched her, his expression more peaceful than it had been in some time. It would always break her heart a little to look at the new white, jagged scar on his brow. She touched it with a finger, swallowing hard.

He's mated with me, she thought, not once, but twice.

I am so lucky. I am the luckiest woman in the world.

The smile she gave him twisted, because it was simply too small of a gesture to contain the enormity of the emotions inside her.

"I love you, you know," she told him.

He cocked a sleek, black eyebrow at her. Coincidentally enough, it was the same brow that now carried the scar. "You surely must, woman."

She chuckled. "Yeah."

Stomach muscles flexing, he sat up and twisted to give her a lingering kiss. "One of the craziest things that has been running through my head," he muttered, "is how goddamned jealous I've been of that other Dragos."

She put her arms around his neck. "Maybe I tried too soon to make you feel better about him. I could have used the threat of him to keep you under control."

Maybe that wasn't a very funny joke, but she was pleased with the effort. Every time they talked, every joke, every revelation, meant they put one more step between them and what had happened.

He must have agreed because he smiled briefly against her lips. Putting a hand at the back of her head, he deepened the kiss, and it escalated swiftly—a hot, explosive flash fire of emotion.

Coming up on his knees, his face taut and flushed with need, he yanked her clothes off. She was a willing participant, wriggling out of her top before he could figure out the complexities of undoing the buttons.

When he kicked off his jean shorts, his hardened penis bounced as it came free of the material. He pulled her down onto the grass and covered her with his body.

They could find time for foreplay and finesse later. Much later, after the first wave of the mating urge eased, or perhaps, for her, after the memory of the fear and pain over the last two days faded.

They weren't there yet. For now, he took her in a blaze of heat, and they coupled like the animals they were. Words tangled with motion, and it all became one thing.

I love you, love you.

I'll never let you go. You're mine. You're my mate.

They burned each other out, until at last they could rest quietly in each other's arms.

At last, he pulled away from her. She watched as he went to the pile of wrapped gold and jewels. Unceremoniously, he dumped the sapphires into her pack, took the cloth that the jewels had been wrapped in and dampened it at the spring.

When he returned, he washed the inside of her thighs gently. She stroked his arm as he did it, marveling at his intent expression. Sometimes he wanted so desperately to get something right, the sight of it shot like an arrow right through her.

After he finished, they dressed. The sky was darkening by the time they packed the rest of his treasure into the pack. He shifted back into his dragon form, invited her into the curve of his paw, and after she had settled comfortably, they flew back to the estate.

Once the buildings came into view, he banked and wheeled overhead, not suspiciously, as he had the day before, but in a more leisurely fashion, as he took a good look in the last light of day.

She glanced without much interest over the scene.

They had flown over many times, just like this, as they talked about plans for renovations and the new buildings. Most of her attention remained on him, as she gauged his reaction to the things he saw.

Which was why she noticed the small hitch in the rhythm of his flight.

He said, curiously, "We never talked about that building."

She looked down again at the focus of his attention.

It was the house of the estate manager, some distance away from the construction site, along the curve of the lake.

A pang struck. Although she wouldn't trade her memories away for anything, it was hard to remember their time together all by herself.

She told him, "It's the estate manager's house. His name is Mitchell. He used to live here full-time when the main house was empty, but he's taking a vacation right now, as we figure out how to restructure his job."

Dragos folded his wings and descended. Even though she knew he would never drop her, the abrupt change in altitude made her clutch at one of his talons.

Landing on the shore of the lake in front of the house, he set her down and shapeshifted. He wore a strained, listening expression.

Watching him, she said, "We spent our wedding night in that house."

He whispered, "You gave birth there. In that room, with the big window, while we looked over the lake. We were all alone."

Her breath stopped, and her heart began to race. "Yes."

He turned on her, with the swiftness of fresh outrage. "You stole one of my pennies!"

She wasn't sure what pure joy looked like.

But she knew what it felt like, shining out of her own face.

Chapter Ten

WHILE HIS FIRST breakthrough was nothing short of miraculous, his recovery was not quite so simple or easy.

They took two more days together, partly so that he could gain some control over the volatility of his mating urges, and partly to see if he might regain more of his memories before they began to deal with the outside world again.

After hours of patiently talking between long bouts of lovemaking, he recalled most of their time together. A few odd bits and pieces still remained missing, but he lost the sense of competing with *the other Dragos*, especially when he recalled the intensity of mating with her the first time.

She was right. She was in his bones. One morning, as they lay exhausted and entwined, he whispered into her hair, "I'll always mate with you."

He could hear the smile in her voice as she whispered back, "I believe you."

Pia managed to convince him that he should have at least one consultation with Dr. Kathryn Shaw, the Wyr surgeon who often treated sentinels when they were injured. Because of that, the doctor was privy to certain confidences.

Although he finally agreed, Dragos was reluctant to do even that. Secretive by nature, it went against a very strong instinct in him to reveal to anyone the fact that his memory still remained impaired.

The morning of the consultation, Graydon brought Kathryn to the house. She was another avian Wyr, a falcon, and they flew in to land in the clearing, shapeshifted into their human forms and stood talking together for a few minutes before walking up to the front door.

They were the first people to return to the estate. Their arrival had been carefully choreographed, with nothing left to chance, so that Dragos could observe both of them from a distance.

When he laid eyes on Graydon's brawny figure, Dragos said immediately, "Of course, I know him. He is a good friend of mine—one of my best friends—and we've worked together for centuries."

Pia's expression lit up all over again. "You absolutely have."

When Dragos switched his attention to Kathryn, his frustration returned.

Like most Wyr falcons, the doctor had a nervy, slender form. Her large, honey brown eyes were sharp with intelligence, and she had thick chestnut hair, which she wore pinned away from her narrow face with a plain tortoiseshell barrette.

At Pia's inquiring glance, he said, "I'm supposed to

know her too."

She responded as though he had actually asked a question. "Yes. She's part of our extended inner circle, and she's one of the few people who knows what my Wyr form is. Between her surgery skills and my healing ability, we managed to save Aryal's wings after she'd been badly hurt earlier this year."

Aryal was one of his sentinels, the contentious one. He and Pia had gone over everything she knew about the sentinels the night before.

His mouth tightened. "I've got nothing."

"That's okay." Pia laid a hand on his arm, and he calmed. He always calmed when she touched him. "Will you still let her examine you? Please?"

If the doctor knew about Pia's Wyr form, Dragos could deal with her knowing about him too. "Yes."

She leaned out the front door and waved her arm in invitation, and Graydon and Kathryn approached.

As they drew close, they slowed. At their uncertain expressions, Dragos said to the doctor, "Not you." He looked into Graydon's familiar gray eyes and smiled. "Yes, you."

A broad, relieved grin broke over Graydon's rugged features. As the other man stepped forward, Dragos pulled him into a quick, hard hug.

After letting him go, Graydon made as if he might hug Pia too, but she stepped away nimbly with a warning smile, at which he caught himself up with a sheepish expression.

Dragos had room to be grateful for her quick thinking at maintaining some distance between her and the other man. Wyr could be dangerously volatile when they were in the middle of mating, and in so many ways, he was still a stranger to himself.

Dragos and Pia had cleaned up the broken glass in his office and taped the open window with a covering of thick plastic, so the doctor examined him there.

Graydon went to the kitchen to wait, while Pia remained close by Dragos's side as Kathryn shone a bright penlight into his eyes, tested his reflexes and balance, and asked him a series of questions.

She took care to ask before she did anything, which helped. After getting his assent, she also examined him magically.

Gritting his teeth, he endured the sensation of alien magic sweeping through his head. She was clearly adept at handling injured Wyr with uncertain control over their more violent impulses, and she finished that part of the examination quickly.

Afterward, the doctor perched a hip on the edge of the nearby mahogany table and regarded them with calm, intelligent eyes.

"You already know I'm a surgeon and not a neurologist," Kathryn said. "So my first advice is, we should find you someone who specializes in treating patients with amnesia."

"No," Dragos said. Beside him, Pia stirred. They held hands, and he clamped his fingers tightly over hers. He told her again, "No. It's hard enough for me to trust Kathryn with this. I will not consult with a total stranger."

Pia's shoulders slumped, and she sighed, although she didn't look surprised.

Neither did Kathryn. "Let me know if you revisit that decision," the doctor said. "In the meantime, treating memory loss is as much an art as it is a science, but we do know some things. For example, different types of memory are stored in different ways. Your procedural memory, which involves skills and tasks, appears to be undamaged. You know how to take a shower, how to fly, how to get dressed, etc."

Unexpectedly, one corner of Dragos's mouth quirked. He said, deadpan, "Or how to ride a bicycle."

He felt, rather than saw, Pia's attention flash to him. An exhalation of laughter escaped her, as she shifted in her chair.

"Exactly," said Kathryn. "Then there's declarative memory, which has two parts—semantic and episodic. Semantic memory contains facts and concepts. Episodic memory contains events and experiences. From what you've said, most of your semantic memory appears to be undamaged, but not all of it. You retain many concepts and facts, but the more closely those are tied to your episodic memory—or your events and experiences—the more likely there might be some impairment."

As wordy as that was, it was starting to sound a lot like Pia's *complicated concepts*.

"Explain," he ordered.

"Okay." Kathryn's reply was easygoing enough. She exchanged a glance with Pia and shifted into a more settled position. "You know there is the Wyr demesne here in New York."

"Yes, but I didn't recall that a few days ago." He thought of the wounded dragon resting on the ledge while waiting for a suicidal fool to climb up to him. "I was pretty deep into my animal nature."

"You've done a lot of healing since then." Kathryn hesitated and glanced at Pia again. "I'm going to ask you a question, and I want you to respond quickly, without giving it too much thought. How is the relationship between the Wyr demesne and the Dark Fae demesne?"

"Not bad," he said instantly, then he paused and frowned. "But that wasn't always true, was it?"

"No," Pia said. "It wasn't."

He looked at her from under lowered brows. "What happened?"

Her expression turned wry. "You and the Dark Fae King Urien didn't get along. Urien kidnapped me, and you killed him. But we love the new queen, Niniane."

Kathryn held up one slim hand. "So, on the one hand, you have the semantic memory, or the facts and concepts—which is, the Wyr demesne and the Dark Fae demesne haven't always gotten along." The doctor held up her other hand. "Here, on the other hand, you have episodic memory, or your events and experiences— which is, you killed the Dark Fae King. Both of these are housed in the declarative part of your memory. The damage you've sustained is in that area."

Frustration welled again. Letting go of Pia's hand, he raked his fingers through his hair. He said, "What you're really saying is I might not remember certain facts and concepts if I've got some sort of personal event attached to it?"

"Yes," replied Kathryn. "I think that's likely."

Which meant he might not remember old enemies or secrets that had been hidden long ago.

Inside, the dragon roused as he realized the world around him had gotten that much more dangerous.

Clearly thinking along the same lines, Pia muttered faintly, "Dragos has lived for millennia. He's witnessed and interacted with so much history."

The doctor said again, "Well, yes." Kathryn looked at Dragos. "If it's any consolation, I'm not sure how much a specialist could help you anyway. You have a… unique and capacious mind."

"I've got to get those memories back," he growled. "All of them."

"I'm sorry." Kathryn frowned. "There's no easy way to say this. You did sustain brain damage. It's real and discernible, and I could sense it as a shadowed area when I scanned you. It's very possible the only reason why you've made as much progress as you have is because Pia is the one who healed you. I've seen the kind of miracle that can come from her healing."

He lowered his hands and gave Pia a grim look. She whispered, "We're lucky you're alive, and you remember as much as you do."

Lucky.

Slipping an arm around her shoulders, he leaned his forehead against hers.

Early that morning, in the first blush of dawn, he had speared into her body as she cried out his name, and he had been incredulous at the newness, the raw magnificence of it.

Yes, he was so damned lucky. More lucky than he ever deserved.

After a moment, Kathryn said, "There's another important aspect of memory—emotion. The most vivid memories tend to be tied to emotion, so it's possible those might come back the easiest. Imagery can also be used to stimulate further recall."

As Dragos turned his attention back to the doctor, his eyes narrowed. "Pia told me about Graydon, but I didn't remember him until I saw him."

"That's a great example," Kathryn replied. "I suggest you go through all the photo albums you own. I can also put together some exercises that might help. Just remember, having someone remind you of an event—like killing the Dark Fae King—won't stimulate true recall. But, now that you've started to remember some things, I think you can hope for more periods of spontaneous recovery."

"Yet there's no guarantee I'll get it all back," Dragos said.

Kathryn smiled. "No, but life doesn't come with any guarantees, does it? Your recovery has already been pretty astonishing. Try to be patient and give your brain time to reroute new pathways. You never know what you might be able to achieve."

There was truth in that. He had a mate and a son.

And he remembered a time when he never thought he would have either.

He met Pia's gaze.

She mouthed at him, "Lucky."

His lips tightened, but then he smiled and nodded.

AFTER STAYING FOR another half an hour or so, Kathryn left, with a promise to return for a follow-up exam the following week.

Graydon sent for the rest of the sentinels, and afterward, the two men went out to the patio area, while Pia wandered off to make another phone call.

Graydon carried two bottles of cold beer from the kitchen. They had begun to sweat in the heat of the day. He handed one to Dragos, who inspected the label.

Oh, yes. He liked this beer.

He took a long pull, while Graydon sat forward and leaned his elbows on his knees. "They'll be here in a few," Graydon said. "They were hanging out at a dive bar in town."

Dragos tested out a few words. "Who… got the short straw?"

Graydon's head came up, a smile lightening his craggy features. "Grym stayed in New York."

Grym.

Scowling, Dragos tried and failed to recall what that sentinel looked like.

Graydon promised, "Maybe you have to see him, like you did with me. We'll Skype with him later."

His jaw tightened. "Kathryn said I might not get everything back. That means you and the others need to be extra vigilant, because the gods only know what I won't recall."

Straightening, the other man took a long, deep breath. "Okay," he said. "We'll handle it. We'll teach you everything we know."

"And we need to keep this quiet," Dragos said. "The last thing we need is for this to leak out."

Graydon rubbed the back of his neck. "A lot of people were at the construction site, and news of the accident has already gotten out to the public. But the only ones who know you lost your memory are the sentinels, and the doc." His frowning gray gaze met Dragos's. "It might take some fancy tap dancing, but we can keep this under wraps."

Pia came into sight, and both men paused to look at her. She had her head bowed, as she concentrated on the person on the other end of the phone.

Graydon said in a quiet, telepathic voice, *When you disappeared, she handled things like a boss. She got a plan in place that covered everything—she coordinated the search for you and even drew up a will. Just in case. Then she climbed up that mountain and healed your ass. It was a good thing she was around to save the day.*

As she glanced toward them, Dragos smiled at her.

He said aloud, "Pia saves me every day."

"Amen to that," said Graydon.

They clinked bottles.

Pia hung up and walked over to them. She looked both excited and worried at once.

Dragos stood. "What is it?"

"Liam's going to be here in a few minutes." She bit her lip. "They're driving in with the sentinels. Eva said to be braced."

"What does that mean?"

Her worried expression deepened as she lifted her shoulders. "I don't know! All she would say is that he went through another growth spurt."

Together, they both turned to stare at Graydon, who winced at them apologetically. "Nothing's wrong." He held up both hands. "Liam is fine. So we decided it was best to not disturb you, until you had the capacity to deal with it."

"Deal with what?" Dragos demanded.

His sharp hearing caught the sound of approaching vehicles, so without waiting to hear a reply, he strode through the house, Pia close on his heels.

Two SUVs pulled to a stop, containing Eva and Hugh, and five tall, strong-looking people, all of whom Dragos knew immediately.

Aryal and Quentin. Bayne, Constantine, and Alex.

All his sentinels, except for Grym, who had drawn the short straw and stayed in the city.

Pushing past him, Pia ran down the steps toward the SUV that carried Eva and Hugh. Belatedly, Dragos realized that what he had taken for a space in the backseat was actually filled with a car seat.

Of course it was.

Eva leaped out of the passenger seat, one hand held out toward Pia. "He's all right, it's all right. Aw, shit, there's no way to make this easier."

"What the hell?" Pia exclaimed at her angrily. She pushed past Eva and yanked open the rear door to look inside.

Silence fell over the group, as they stood watching, all except for Dragos, who strode rapidly toward the SUV. His stomach clenched as Pia whispered, "Oh, my God."

She reached into the backseat and lifted out a smiling, tow-headed boy.

A big, beautiful boy. A much bigger boy than the toddler Dragos remembered. He was no expert on children, but Liam looked to be twice as big, maybe four years old.

"What the fuck?" he whispered.

Pia sank to her knees, hugging Liam tight, and the boy threw his arms around her neck. "What did I miss?" she cried. "What did I miss?"

"I missed you," Liam told her. "Bunches and bunches. Hi, Mom."

The boy *talked*.

Reaching their side, Dragos sank to his knees beside them.

"Look at you," Pia breathed. She ran her hands compulsively over Liam. "How did this happen?"

Liam beamed. "I'm being a big soldier."

Her eyes went wide, and she looked as if she'd been punched.

The boy cocked his head, and his smile started to dim. "Isn't that what you wanted?"

Immediately she snatched him tight, kissing him all over his face and hugging him fiercely, as she sobbed, "Of course it is. You're such a *good, good boy*. You're the most amazing boy I've ever seen. It's okay to stop growing now. It really is. You can stop for a while. Dear God, you're big enough."

Liam kissed her back then turned his attention to Dragos and grew still.

Sensing Liam's change in focus, Pia looked at Dragos, too. With obvious reluctance, she let her arms loosen and let Liam stand on his own.

Dragos wanted to reach for him, but Liam hung back, leaning against his mom.

Dragos asked, "Are you afraid of me?"

Shaking his head, the boy asked a question of his own. "Do you remember me?"

"I do," he said, a little hoarsely. "I remember you so well, and I really don't want you to be afraid of me."

Liam pushed away from Pia and stepped toward him. Holding very still, Dragos watched many expressions pass over that young face.

Liam looked into his gaze. It was an old, deep look from those violet eyes, a look that did not seem to come from a child.

Then Liam smiled and patted him on the cheek.

He said in a gentle voice, "You're a good dad."

Astonished, broken wide open, Dragos felt something slide down his face. He touched his cheek and discovered wetness. Feeling a fullness and depth of emotion he had never felt before, he watched as Liam slipped around him and skipped toward the house.

Thank you!

Dear Readers,

Thank you for reading my novella, *Pia Saves the Day*. Dragos, Pia and Peanut are some of my favorite characters, and I'm delighted to share this new story with you. I hope you have as much fun visiting with them as I did!

Would you like to stay in touch and hear about new releases? You can:

- Sign up for my newsletter at: www.theaharrison.com
- Follow me on Twitter at @TheaHarrison
- Like my Facebook page at facebook.com/TheaHarrison

Reviews help other readers find the books they like to read. I appreciate each and every review, whether positive or negative.

Pia Saves the Day is the second story in a three-story arc featuring Dragos, Pia and their son Peanut. The first story is *Dragos Takes a Holiday*, and the third is *Peanut Goes to School*. While each story is written so that it can be enjoyed individually, the reading experience will be stronger if you enjoy all three in order.

Happy reading!
Thea

Now Available

Dragos Takes a Holiday

(A novella of the Elder Races)

The Bermuda Triangle. Pirates. The Peanut. What could possibly go wrong?

Dragos Cuelebre needs a vacation. So does Pia, his mate. When the First Family of the Wyr head to Bermuda for some much needed R&R, it's no ordinary undertaking – and no ordinary weekend in the sun. Between hunting for ancient treasure buried beneath the waves and keeping track of their son, Liam—a.k.a. Peanut, whose Wyr abilities are manifesting far ahead of schedule—it's a miracle that Pia and Dragos can get any time together.

They're determined to make the most of each moment, no matter who tries to get in their way.

And did we mention pirates?

For fans of *Dragon Bound* and *Lord's Fall*, passion, playfulness, and adventure abound in this Elder Races novella.

Dragos Takes a Holiday is part of a three-story series about Pia, Dragos, and Peanut. Each story stands alone, but fans might want to read all three: *Dragos Takes a Holiday*, *Pia Saves the Day*, and *Peanut Goes to School*.

Look for these titles from Thea Harrison

THE ELDER RACES SERIES – FULL LENGTH NOVELS

Published by Berkley

Dragon Bound

Storm's Heart

Serpent's Kiss

Oracle's Moon

Lord's Fall

Kinked

Night's Honor

Midnight's Kiss

Shadow's End

ELDER RACES NOVELLAS

True Colors

Natural Evil

Devil's Gate

Hunter's Season

The Wicked

Dragos Takes a Holiday

Pia Saves the Day

Peanut Goes to School

Dragos Goes to Washington

Pia Does Hollywood

Liam Takes Manhattan

GAME OF SHADOWS SERIES

Published by Berkley

Rising Darkness

Falling Light

ROMANCES UNDER THE NAME AMANDA CARPENTER

E-published by Samhain Publishing
(original publication by Harlequin Mills & Boon)

A Deeper Dimension

The Wall

A Damaged Trust

The Great Escape

Flashback

Rage

Waking Up

Rose-Coloured Love

Reckless

The Gift of Happiness

Caprice

Passage of the Night

Cry Wolf

A Solitary Heart

The Winter King

Printed in Great Britain
by Amazon